No Tree, No We

Orange Books Publication

1st Floor, Rajhans Arcade, Mall Road, Kohka, Bhilai, Chhattisgarh 490020

Website: **www.orangebooks.in**

© **Copyright, 2024, Author**

All rights reserved. No part of this book may be reproduced, stored in a retrieval system, or transmitted, in any form by any means, electronic, mechanical, magnetic, optical, chemical, manual, photocopying, recording or otherwise, without the prior written consent of its writer.

First Edition, 2024
ISBN: 978-93-5621-549-8

No Tree No We

THANGJAM RAMANANDA SINGH

Orange Books Publication
www.orangebooks.in

Content

Chapter - 1
    The Village of Thangmeiband 1

Chapter - 2
    The Bond with the Teak Tree 12

Chapter - 3
    The Disappearance of the Teak Tree 23

Chapter - 4
    Life in Imphal City 34

Chapter - 5
    The Mysterious Neighbours 54

Chapter – 6
    Dark Revelations 63

Chapter – 7
    Recognizing the Need for Power 71

Chapter - 8
    Confrontation with Illegal Loggers 82
    Conclusion 96

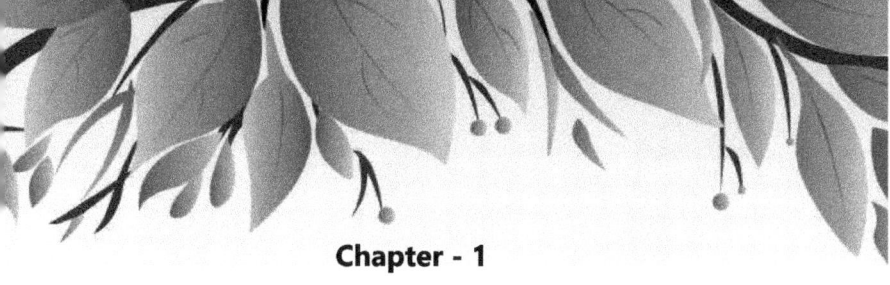

Chapter - 1

The Village of Thangmeiband

Thangmeiband Village, located in Manipur, is a calm and peaceful place surrounded by the beautiful Cheirou Ching woodland. The village is home to about 200 residents who live in simple but sturdy thatch and bamboo houses. In Thangmeiband Village, life is all about simplicity and living in harmony with nature. The villagers follow the natural patterns of the seasons and agricultural cycles in their daily lives. The people in Thangmeiband Village are famous for being really close and having old-fashioned beliefs. They all help each other with farming, taking care of animals, and doing cool things that show off their culture. In the village, there are many skilled artists who create amazing crafts, using traditional techniques that have been passed down through generations.

When you go to Thangmeiband Village, you can try yummy Manipuri food that's super tasty and made with local ingredients. You can also watch cool dance shows, listen to music, and enjoy other cultural stuff that shows off the region's awesome heritage.

The people in Thangmeiband village were really close. They had families that had been there for a long time. Many generations had lived and done well in the village, so they felt that they really belonged there. Everyone knew each other's names and they trusted and respected each other. When something good happened, they celebrated together. And when things were tough, they all came together to help and comfort each other. The families in Thangmeiband village were so close that nothing could break their bond. They were like one big family, and that was something really amazing. In Thangmeiband, the people relied on agriculture for their living... The soil in the fields was really good for growing different kinds of crops like rice, veggies, and pulses. Everyone in the community worked together to plow the fields, plant the seeds, and gather the crops. It was a team effort for them to make farming successful.

Peasants in Thangmeiband had different ways to earn money besides farming. Some helped with buildings or road maintenance, while others were skilled at making tools, baskets, or pottery. Some gathered firewood, honey, and herbs to sell at the market. The locals started their day by caring for their animals or fields, and women chatting near the well, while getting water. Kids learned traditions from their parents, and everyone came together for festivals and celebrations, like the harvest festival, which was full of eating, dancing, and singing. They also honored earth, wood and land gods for a good crop and prosperity. Thangmeiband village faced several issues despite its beautiful surroundings. Natural disasters like floods and droughts would ruin the crops and disrupt the village's way of life. Also, lots of young people were leaving for the nearby cities which was making things tough. Modern development was taking place gradually but it was also kind of threatening the old-fashioned ways. The villagers were trying to figure out ways to keep their traditions alive at the same time accepting changes that were taking place... Some people wanted more money for schools and roads to help the kids attain better opportunities. Others wanted things to remain the same because they were worried that probably too many changes might mess up the special balance between nature and people, as they had been working for them for a long time.

Ade lived with his family in the calm village of Thangmeiband. Their small wooden house, surrounded by the tall trees of Cheirou Ching woodland and vast fields, was their comfy home. Ade, the youngest in the family, was a happy twelve-year-old boy. He was always excited to discover the amazing things in nature. He would spend his days exploring the forest, listening to the sound of the leaves and birds. Ade had a unique connection with the trees and animals in the woods. They trusted him and would always follow him, wherever he went. Even though Ade's family lived a simple life in Thangmeiband, they were happy and satisfied. Ade's parents worked tirelessly, to take care of their kids. Every night, they would sit by the fireplace, telling stories laughing together and making memories that would stay with them forever. Ade's dad, Mr. Jackson, wasn't just an ordinary farmer; he was a man who worked with all his heart and soul. He started early in the morning and didn't stop until the sun went down, taking care of the crops with a lot of dedication.

Mr. Jackson wasn't only good at farming; he was also a kind-hearted person. He cared deeply for his family and the land, he cultivated. He considered the planet a valuable gift and took great care of it. Mrs. Thoinu, Ade's mom, was always gentle and kind, unlike Mr. Jackson who appeared tough on the outside. She created a warm and a secure atmosphere in their house, like a comforting embrace that filled everyone's heart with love. Mrs. Thoinu was really good at the art of using words to make people feel better. She was so nice and caring that everyone would go to her, for help and support. She had this amazing talent to understand what others needed and would always be there to listen and support them. Her words were like magic, making people feel calm and happy. She loved her family very much. Ade had an elder brother named Ryan, who was two years older than him. Ryan was a quiet kid who liked to read books, unlike Ade, who liked to go outside, chase butterflies, and climb trees. Even though Ade and Ryan were not alike, they had a close connection as brothers. Their different hobbies didn't stop them from being friends; it actually made their friendship even stronger... Ade would always come back from his adventures with some cool stuff or cool stories and that would make Ryan super excited.

Their parents, aware of their talents and preferences, encouraged both boys to pursue their aspirations. Ade's parents enrolled him in nature camps and consistently motivated him to inquire about the world. On the other hand, they provided numerous books for Ryan to read and constantly encouraged him whenever he penned stories. Love and laughter united them to create a beautiful family. Ade's family possessed true wealth in the form of love, laughter, and the splendor of nature, even in the face of difficulties. The large forest surrounding their village was filled with old trees that stood tall and strong, resembling vigilant guards protecting their land and had become a big part of their lives. They got wood to build their homes and also picked fruits and veggies from there... Ade loved exploring the forest, amazed by all the beauty and magic that he found there. The forest was also a scary and an unknown place. Ade's parents warned him not to go too far from home because they were worried, he might get lost or encounter wild animals. However, Ade was a curious kid and couldn't resist the excitement of exploring.

Mother: "Ade, please be careful when you go into the woodland. It can be dangerous and full of mysteries that might scare you."

Ade: "I know, Mom, but I can't resist exploring. I promise to stay close to home and will also be cautious."

Mother: "I understand your curiosity, but remember to listen to your instincts and come back if you feel unsafe."

Ade: "Don't worry, Mom. I'll be careful."

The Jackson family lived in the heart of Thangmeiband Village, where the dense Cheirou Ching forest encroached upon the village's edge. Their simple bamboo and thatch house was hidden among the towering trees, showing their strong connection to the nature around them.

Every morning, as the sun started to shine through the trees, Ade and his father would explore the forest. They ventured into the forest to gather firewood for cooking and heating their house. Meanwhile, Thoinu would lead Ade deeper into the forest, teaching him about the healing properties of various herbs and plants. With her sharp eyes and gentle touch, she would identify and collect a wide range of therapeutic treasures, from fragrant leaves to vibrant flowers, and thus passing down the ancient knowledge of their ancestors to Ade. The forest had lots of yummy food like berries, shoots, and mushrooms. Ade loved exploring the forest and finding these tasty treats. It made him realize, how everything in nature is connected and he felt really thankful for all the good stuff, the forest gave to them...

This twelve-year-old kid named Ade was really curious about everything. He had a tremendous desire to be adventurous. The Cheirou Ching jungle, with its dense trees, seemed to be whispering secrets to the wind. Ade couldn't wait to discover the amazing things hidden in the jungle. With excitement, he started walking into the jungle, feeling happy and excited. He spotted many different animals and plants, as he ventured deeper into the forest; some were scary, and some were fascinating. He laughed at the amusing behavior of the monkeys, as they hopped from one branch to another. Birds of different shapes and sizes sang in unison, as they glided through the trees. He was in awe of the vast array of life surrounding him, each living being was a perfect example of the incredible diversity, of the jungle.

He thought that the trees communicated with him, by the sound of the leaves and moving branches; their voices were soft and warm, similar to the whispers of a wise old man. He found hidden gems in the bushes, as he continued his journey through the forest. The wildflowers bloomed in a burst of colors, their petals shining with dew. Mushrooms sprouted from the damp soil, each one unique in shape and size. He happily collected these treasures, while marveling at the abundance and beauty of nature. His eyes were filled with wonder and excitement, with every step that he took. He listened to the secrets whispered by the gentle rustling of leaves and the intricate patterns of sunlight on the forest floor.

Stepping out of the woods, he realized that his journey had transformed him permanently. His heart was filled with awe and joy. He realized that the world was full of endless wonders and secrets. Every tree and creature had a special story to share. He learned that the most incredible moments were not found in distant lands or daring adventures, but in the quiet moments of discovery and understanding. It was like the world was a hidden treasure, just waiting to be explored.

Ade's mind was filled with the sounds and sights of the jungle, as he made his way towards Thangmeiband Village. He realized that his adventure was not over yet. There were more puzzles to unravel, peaks to conquer, and streams to cross. He embarked on the unexplored land once again, filled with a renewed determination to keep discovering and gaining knowledge.

Ade continued to explore deeper into the Cheirou Ching forest, as the sun sank beneath the horizon, creating elongated shadows on the ground. He had been told about a stunning teak tree, with branches that stretched high into the sky, located right in the center of the forest. Intrigued by the stories, he was determined to find the tree and solve its secrets by himself.

He kept going, feeling his heart beat faster with excitement, following the gentle sound of leaves and the faint glow of fireflies moving around the trees. He carefully made his way through the tangled vines and narrow paths, keeping a close eye on everything around him. After what felt like hours of walking, he finally arrived at a clearing bathed in the soft glow of the moonlight. And there it stood, the majestic Teak Tree, proud and magnificent, right before his eyes.

He looked up at the huge tree, its branches stretching out like a green umbrella, its trunk as thick as a giant's arm, and he couldn't breathe. He felt a deep respect for the Teak Tree. He moved closer and reached out his hand to touch the rough bark, sensing the vibrant energy flowing beneath his touch. He couldn't believe it, when he felt a strange tingly sensation shoot up his arm, as soon as he touched the tree. It was as if the tree was talking to him in a secret language, that only they could understand. Even though he was a bit scared, he didn't give up. He bravely moved closer and pressed his ear against the rough bark, hoping to hear the mysterious voice of the tree.

Out of nowhere, he heard a soft, musical voice speaking in his ear, sharing wise advice and guidance with him, like a calm wind moving through the trees. The ancient and wise Teak Tree was communicating with him in a language that couldn't be described.

The tree whispered, "Hello, little one." its voice sounding like the gentle rustling of leaves in the wind. "I knew you would come."

He couldn't believe his eyes, when he saw the tree talking directly to him! His eyes got really big because he was so surprised. Even though his grandma had told him stories about trees that could talk, he never thought he would actually see one in real life. The tree spoke with a soothing and comforting tone, giving him the impression that it possessed great wisdom and had existed for a considerable period. It told him about how everything in nature is connected and how there is a beautiful balance in the world.

The tree told tales about the animals, that lived in the forest. It talked about the squirrels that danced on the branches, the birds that sang in the treetops, and the deer that peacefully ate in the meadows. Every creature had an important part in maintaining the balance of the ecosystem, and the tree was thankful to them.

"You are a guardian of this sacred place," the tree said, its voice filled with reverence. "Your presence brings light and joy, to all who dwell here. May you continue to walk this path with love and compassion in your heart, for the forest is a reflection of your own inner beauty."

And when the sun started to go down, making the treetops shine with a golden light, the tree stood tall and strong, like a quiet guard protecting the forest and its dear friends. Their bond was so strong, it couldn't be broken, even by time and distance. And when the night came, and the stars sparkled above the tree softly whispered a last message of love and thanks before falling into a peaceful sleep.

When the tree spoke, a feeling of warmth spread through his body, making his heart swell with gratitude and humility. Even though he had already felt connected to nature but listening to the Teak Tree speak so lovingly about him, filled him with a newfound sense of purpose.

The tree grew serious in its warning, "But beware, young one." "A threat unlike anything the forest has ever faced is approaching, and darkness is quickly closing in"." The destiny of the forest is with you, so you must be brave and strong."

Ade became worried, when the tree gave a warning. He had heard about deforestation near Thangmeiband Village, but he never thought it could harm their forest. Determined and brave, he stood tall and looked directly into the tree's eyes, ready to do whatever it would take to protect the beloved forest.

Ade spoke with determination, "I promise to do everything that is possible to keep the forest safe and all the creatures living. "I won't give up, no matter what it takes, to make sure the forest remains beautiful and magical forever."

The Teak Tree moved its branches gently, showing its support, as it nodded in agreement. "You are so smart for your age," it whispered to itself. "You will overcome any challenge with courage and determination. Remember, the forest is a special place, full of life and beauty that we must protect and cherish, and not just a home for trees and animals."

Ade walked away from the teak tree and entered the dark night, feeling a strong sense of purpose in his heart. The words he had heard, kept repeating in his mind. He knew that the journey ahead would not be easy, but he was ready to face all the challenges that would come in his way. With the wisdom of the teak tree to guide him, Ade disappeared into the shadows, promising to protect the forest and everyone living in it. His destiny pushed him deeper into the unknown.

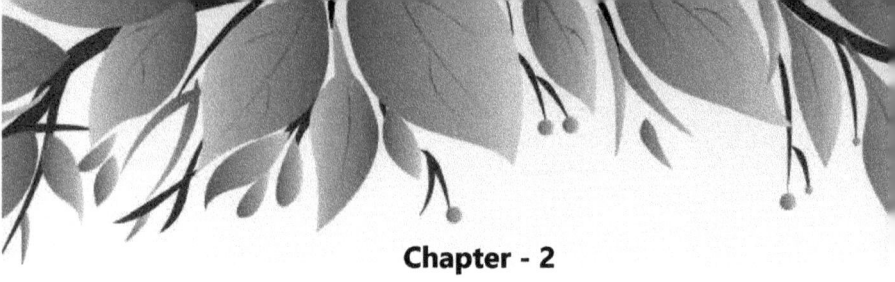

Chapter - 2

The Bond with the Teak Tree

Ade felt a strong pull towards the forest after meeting the talking Teak Tree, and he was unable to stay away from its charm. Every day, he went back to the woods, filled with happiness and wonder at the surprises hidden among the trees and leaves. Among the many beautiful trees in the forest, there was one that Ade loved the most: the Teak Tree. Despite its simple look, the Teak Tree had a unique charm that fascinated Ade. He felt a strong bond with the tick tree. It felt like the tree had a special purpose in his life.

Ade always made sure to find the Teak tree, every time he went to the forest. He followed a secret path of familiarity and love that showed him the way. Sitting under its branches, he loved the peacefulness it brought and felt a comforting calmness all around him. He felt calm and protected by the Teak Tree's shelter. It was a special place where he could just hide from the troubles of the world. The Teak Tree was different from the rest of the trees in the forest because it was right on the edge of a small open space. Its leaves sparkled in the sun like shiny gold droplets, and its twisted branches looked like the arms of a familiar old friend. As time passed, he felt a strange bond forming between him and the tree, as if, it was silently beckoning him to come closer.

Ade was filled with a lot of excitement as he made his way to the teak Ttee. Even though he had walked on this path countless times before, he couldn't get away with the feeling that something incredible was about to occur. Ade's trip to the teak Ttree wasn't just a walk in the woods. It felt like a magical mission, a sacred adventure to a mysterious spot. With every step that Ade took, he felt a stronger connection towards the heart of the forest, his senses heightened at the incredible beauty of nature.

Ade's heart was filled with excitement, as he got closer to the famous open area, where the teak tree stood tall... He couldn't help but feel a surge of happiness, making him breathe faster. Every time he went to the teak tree, it felt like a brand -new adventure. He could feel the magic of nature and a special bond with something that was greater than him. Each meeting left him amazed and thrilled, as if the tree held all the secrets of the universe in its old branches. He was so excited and couldn't wait to start exploring the Teak Tree. The forest was full of amazing things to discover and he was ready for another thrilling adventure.

Ade walked up to the tree and reached out to feel the rough bark he knew so well. "Hi, old friend," he murmured quietly. "Good to see you again."

Despite his surprise, he continued moving forward and moved closer. He leaned his ear against the rough bark, listening attentively for any sign of the enigmatic tree's voice. He was surprised when he heard a soft, musical voice speaking in his ear, like a gentle wind moving through the trees. The ancient and wise teak tree's voice reached him, communicating in a language that went beyond words.

The tree whispered, "Hey Ade, it's nice to see you back," sounding like the wind rustling through the leaves. "I've been eagerly anticipating your return!"

"Hey Ade," the Teak Tree said, "you're not just a regular boy. You have a special role as the forest's protector and the guardian of all its creatures."

Ade's heart raced with excitement as he struggled to understand the words he had just heard. He had always felt a deep connection to nature, a sense of belonging that he couldn't quite explain. But to be chosen as the forest's protector? He couldn't have imagined anything like it. As he stood there, the teak tree continued to speak, its voice filled with comfort and encouragement.

It told Ade of the ancient bond between humans and nature, a bond that had been forgotten by many. It explained that Ade possessed a unique gift, a deep empathy and understanding of the forest. The teak tree showed that Ade's job was to make sure the forest was peaceful and balanced. Ade had to keep the delicate ecosystems safe and take care of all the animals that lived there. Ade was to be a bridge between the human world and the natural world, a guardian who would advocate for the voiceless and defend the vulnerable.

Ade felt a lot of responsibility and thankfulness and he promised to embrace his new role with all his heart and soul. He would dedicate his life to preserving the beauty and wonder of the natural world... He promised to gain knowledge from the forest, to pay attention to its soft words and follow its advice. He dedicated his time to discovering its depths, gaining knowledge from the creatures living there, and tirelessly supporting its protection. He became a voice for the trees, the animals, and the delicate ecosystems that relied on the forest's existence.

Ade and the Teak Tree were really close in the Cheirou Ching forest. Ade and the Teak Tree could still feel each other's presence, even in the pitch-black night when the stars and moon were hidden by the trees. Despite not being able to see each other in the traditional sense, Ade and the Teak Tree knew they were close. During those peaceful times, Ade and the Teak tree discovered comfort in each other's presence. Even during the darkest nights, Ade and the Teak Tree felt reassured by the fact that they were never really alone. The deep connection they formed in the heart of Cheirou Ching forest demonstrated the strength of bonds and the true beauty of nature's embrace.

Even though the forest was distant, he could sense the tree's strong presence, like a reassuring figure in the dark. Despite the darkness and distance between them, their connection remains unbreakable, a testament to their love and friendship. Ade had a dream about the forest, where he heard the leaves rustling, the stream murmuring calmly, and the trees gently swaying, as he drifted off to sleep. In his dream, he felt the presence of the Teak Tree beside him, guarding him as he peacefully slept. Similarly, the Teak Tree shielded the moonlit open space, its branches extending towards the sky. Ade and the Teak Tree became inseparable friends in the heart of the forest, where the trees shared secrets and the shadows danced. Even without seeing each other, they communicated through the rustling leaves and gentle whistling of the wind. Ade always felt a powerful attraction to the peaceful teak tree in the Cheirou Ching forest every morning. The majestic tree stood tall and proud, with its ancient trunk decorated by beautiful designs carved over time.

As time passed, Ade's bond with the Teak Tree became even stronger, their friendship thriving in the lush green forest. Their friendship grew stronger every day as they trusted each other, respected one another, and shared countless special moments. He discovered peace and comfort in the tranquil forest, finding solace in the teak tree's strong and silent presence. They would sit together under the tree's branches, enjoying the calmness of their surroundings and confiding in each other.

As the seasons shifted and the forest underwent a transformation, Ade and the Teak Tree stayed loyal friends, their bond became tighter each day because they believed in each other, admired one another, and made many unforgettable memories together. They tackled life's obstacles side by side, finding comfort in each other's presence and enjoying the joy of nature's little wonders. He was amazed by the beauty and strength of the teak tree every day. As time passed, Ade's relationship with the teak tree grew stouter, and their connection was transforming into something truly enchanting. They laughed and cried together, shared their dreams and fears, aware of the fact that they were united by a force beyond their own existence. Amidst the Cheirou Ching forest, Ade and the Teak Tree formed a strong relationship that would last forever, their friendship growing like a flower in the spring, enduring and timeless.

Ade couldn't resist the Teak Tree's charm, just like a moth can't resist a flame. He followed the sound of the stream and the gentle rustling of the leaves, venturing further into the forest. The Teak Tree stood alone, protecting Ade with a kind loyalty through everything. Ade sensed the tree's presence guiding him like a beacon of light, as he ventured deeper into the forest, taking him on new experiences and discoveries…

Ade opened up to the Teak Tree in ways he had never opened up to anyone before as he spent more time with it. He opened himself to the quiet guardian in front, sharing his anxieties, uncertainties, his hopes and dreams. The Teak Tree understood and listened quietly, its branches gently swaying in the wind like a comforting hug. They created a beautiful tapestry of memories, weaving together stories and secrets that connected them forever. Ade shared with the Teak Tree his childhood tales of climbing the largest tree in the forest, saving an injured bird from a hungry predator, and spending a night dancing under the stars with his pals.

The Teak Tree also told its own stories of long ago, including the rise and fall of entire civilizations, the flow of life and death, and the never-ending cycle of rebirth and renewal. Ade felt his connection to the tree strengthening with each tale, his soul becoming connected with the age-old knowledge that trickled down its limbs like sap.

Ade looked to the Teak Tree for direction and support when he went through difficulties and trials in his life. He would hide beneath its branches when he was doubtful and afraid, and whenever his heart was heavy with anxiety. Ade grew to trust and look up to the Teak Tree as a mentor, providing guidance and support when he needed it most. It helped him develop confidence in his own skills and believe in himself, even when things were uncertain and difficult. Ade found comfort in the teak tree; it was his reliable companion in a chaotic world.

Ade's connection to the forest and all its creatures deepened along with his relationship with the Teak Tree. They rejoiced in the wonders of life and death, as well as the beauty and diversity of the natural world, and they cherished the magnificence of the changing seasons. Ade and the Teak Tree also realized that their friendship would last forever, a monument to the strength of love and connection, as they celebrated their oneness and friendship. Ade had made a lifelong companion in the tall, noble Teak Tree in the center of the Cheirou Ching forest, where the sound of falling leaves filled the air. And so, they would travel through the years together, their spirits entwined like the roots of old trees, united by an unbreakable link.

Ade's family found peace and food in the dense forest of Thangmeiband Village. The giant trees appeared to be keeping countless secrets, murmured by the breeze. For generations, the forest had been a vital source of livelihood and spiritual nourishment. Ade's family felt really worried, when they heard about deforestation. The forest was not only a pretty place for them, but also really important for their survival. Their way of life relied on the forest being healthy and strong, but the approaching destruction was a serious danger to them. When trees are cut down, people's bond with the earth becomes weaker, and the fragile harmony of nature gets messed up.

Ade's family did everything they could to protect the forest, but they couldn't stop the progress from moving forward. Ade's family remained resilient in the face of constant danger of environmental destruction creeping closer to their peaceful home. Despite the uncertainty, they stood united in their mission to safeguard their heritage. They understood that the fight against deforestation would be difficult and lengthy, but they also understood how crucial the situation was. In the calm Thangmeiband Village, surrounded by lush nature, the far-off noise of chainsaws could be heard cutting through the trees, disturbing the peaceful forest sounds. At first, Ade's family and the rest of the forest dwellers ignored thinking of it as just a small noise of progress, the unavoidable invasion of civilization into their special home. But as the never-ending buzzing continued, getting louder and more annoying every day, a feeling of worry started to spread through the village like a shadow.

Yet, as the days stretched into weeks and the weeks into months, the true nature of the threat became impossible to ignore. The sound of chainsaws that were far away before, now sounded closer and closer, filling the forest with their loud noise. Ade's family and the people in Thangmeiband Village started to realize that, deforestation was a bigger problem than they thought, and it made them really worried. The progress that was once ignored as nonsense talk was now seen as a serious danger to how they lived. The forest, where they used to find safety and food, were now being attacked, with the tall trees being cut down without care for the sake of moving forward. Ade's family and the other villagers were really worried when the trees were getting cut down, closer and closer to their homes. They felt like it was a really big problem, they had never dealt with before. Their peaceful life was now filled with worry and fear, as progress kept moving forward and putting their forest in danger.

Ade's family and the other villagers joined forces, determined to safeguard the forest and all its creatures from the advancing wave of destruction. As the days went by, they became more determined and their strength increased, never giving up even when things got tough. They understood that the fight against deforestation would be tough and take a long time, but they also knew that the importance of winning was incredibly high. For them, the forest was not just a collection of trees and wildlife. It was a special place that was important for their survival and success.

Ade's family witnessed personally the devastation as deforestation crept closer to Thangmeiband Village. The disappearance of the trees and the resulting barrenness jeopardized their way of life, which had previously depended on the forest for subsistence. Ade's father, Mr. Jackson, battled to make ends meet while the animals ran away and the crops failed, leaving a barren, lifeless countryside in their wake.

Ade's mom, Mrs. Thoinu, worked really hard to keep their house organized, but when they didn't have enough supplies and things started looking bad, her hard work didn't pay off. Ade's family struggled, yet they never gave up on their dreams. They were aware that they needed to defend the forest, which had provided for them for many generations, and served as their home. They therefore promised to do whatever was required to defend the land they loved, their resolve burning fiercely in their hearts.

Ade's family realized they needed assistance in dealing with the growing threat of deforestation. In order to stand together against a shared foe, they required the assistance of their fellow villages and the power of community. They therefore rallied their friends and neighbors to join the effort to conserve the forest by calling upon them. As a group, they created a coalition of concerned citizens that was formidable in the fight against deforestation. They planned rallies and demonstrations, marching through the streets defiantly waving banners and raising their voices. They filed a petition with the local government, requesting that they take steps to save the forest and maintain its beauty for upcoming generations.

People who wanted to make money by destroying the forest, like greedy developers, corrupt politicians, and selfish businesses, were against, what they were trying to do. They used every possible tactic to make the peasants weaker, like giving money to people in charge, spreading lies, and even being violent to scare their enemies.

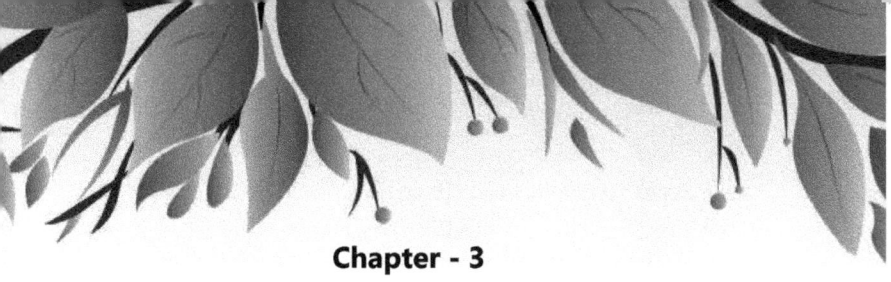

Chapter - 3

The Disappearance of the Teak Tree

In the middle of Thangmeiband Village, surrounded by the huge Cheirou Ching woodland, there was a very important symbol—a grand Teak Tree. This tall and mighty tree, called the "Teak Tree," ruled over the village, showing how strong and wise it was, and reminding everyone of the special connection between people and nature. The people of Thangmeiband Village have long honored the Teak Tree. The Teak Tree held a significant meaning for the villagers, aside from its remarkable size.

The Teak Tree was a powerful symbol of the strong connection between people and nature. It reminded everyone of how much, humans rely on the Earth and the need to protect its fragile ecosystem. The tree had been standing strong for many years, teaching the villagers to care for nature and live in harmony with the land. On that day, the peacefulness of the forest was suddenly disrupted by a disturbing noise. The loud sound of axes chopping wood and the intimidating roar of machines filled the air, showing that humans were encroaching on nature's sacred space. The calm scenery was now ruined by the harsh sounds of development, bringing doubt about the fate of the Teak Tree and the village it protected. The people of Thangmeiband were greatly disturbed by the unexpected invasion of their beloved forest. The peaceful bond they had with nature took a sudden turn. Instead of being happy and respectful, they're now fighting and feeling worried. The axes continued to chop, with each strike bringing a sense of betrayal and violation towards something valuable. Every fallen tree represented a loss of the village's history, as if severing the roots that connected them to their past. The loud noise of machines made the villagers even more worried.

In the middle of all the craziness, the Teak Tree stayed quiet, watching the exciting things happening around it. Despite all the damage, the tree remained strong, showing hope when everything else seemed dark. How long could the Teak Tree endure the invasion of humans? The Teak Tree was highly important to them because it was deeply rooted in their collective identity. Their survival depended on it, so they were committed to safeguarding its heritage for the next generations. As the day began, Ade stepped out of his cozy house as the sun started to shine over the town. The shining light made the forest glow. He was really excited for another day spent under the safe and sheltering branches of the Teak Tree. Since childhood, it had been a source of solace and guidance for him. Ade ventured deeper into the woods, sensing the strong sense of excitement in the air. Ade's heart filled with fear as he ventured into the forest. Finally, he stepped into a tiny open space, revealing the core of the forest in front of him. In that place, surrounded by the destruction, that had ruined the once beautiful scenery, were the broken pieces of his cherished Teak Tree. The massive tree trunk, representing centuries of wisdom and power, now lay broken and still, destroyed by loggers driven by their selfish desire for profit and indifference.

Ade was devastated by what he saw, feeling like everything he cherished had been betrayed. Ade felt really sad when he saw The Teak Tree lying on the ground. It was a tree that many people admired and respected for a long time. Its tall height gave people a cozy place to rest under its shade. Ade felt really miserable when he felt the pain of all the people who had admired the Teak Tree. Their voices were stopped by the unstoppable progress. He was not only sad about losing something important, but also about the disturbance of the delicate balance between people and nature, a bond that had helped civilizations for a long time. Ade felt really weak when he saw the ruined place, understanding how much damage had been done. But then, he suddenly felt a strong desire to remember the Teak Tree and keep the rest of nature safe. Ade promised to always stand up for those, who couldn't speak for themselves and protect the Earth from people who wanted to hurt it, just to make themselves richer. Ade approached the fallen tree and gently touched its rough bark, feeling tears forming in his eyes. When he touched the rough surface with his fingers, he quickly pulled his hand back as if he got a big surprise. The tree was once so tall and beautiful, but now it's all broken up with its branches all over the place. He couldn't understand how much he had lost - for himself, the town, and the forest that had kept them safe for many years. He felt flooded with memories, from the times he spent under the huge tree's branches.

He remembered the private talks held under its branches; the quiet secrets shared among the rustling leaves. Ade found comfort under the Teak Tree not just during peaceful times. He remembered the strong storms that swept through the forest, causing chaos on the ground. During those scary times, the Teak Tree remained sturdy, offering protection from the strong wind and rain. Ade found a peaceful sanctuary under the tree's sheltering branches, where worries faded away and uncertainty was replaced by confidence. Ade couldn't escape the heavy sorrow that now surrounded him, despite the fond memories of friendship and safety. The vibrant group of people who had gathered under the Teak Tree's friendly shade were now separated; their voices taken away by a mean twist of fate. With the tree gone, there was only a vacant spot that echoed with sad memories from before. The Teak Tree, autumn was a gentle reminder of how fragile life can be and how everything is impermanent. It demonstrated that the strongest trees can be defeated by the unstoppable passage of time.

Ade found a tiny spark of hope in the midst of his shattered dreams, a little beam of light to guide him out of the darkness. Even though the Teak Tree is no longer around, its beauty still lives on in the memories of those who saw it. Ade promised to keep the memory of the Teak Tree and the people it helped alive, making sure that its spirit would live on for years to come. Ade will always remember the Teak Tree - the quiet guard that has protected the land for many years. Even though the Teak

Tree disappeared, everyone who had known and loved it still kept its memory alive in their hearts. In the end, it wasn't only a tree that fell down, but a special friend who will always live in the Thangmeiband Village forests, watching over and taking care of everyone, who lives there.

When the Teak Tree was uprooted from its home in the forest and taken to the city, Ade felt a mix of different feelings spinning around inside him. It felt like a piece of him was ripped out, making him feel really sad and like something was missing. Ade's first reaction to the news of the Teak Tree being taken to the city was one of utter devastation. He couldn't understand the idea of his dear friend Teak Tree being taken away from its home in the forest, where it had been for many years, and moved to a strange and unwelcoming place. Ade felt really hurt, gloomy and hopeless when the people took away the Teak Tree from where it belonged. He couldn't understand why someone would be so heartless and would want to upset the fragile harmony of nature in the woods, just to fulfill their own greedy wishes.

He felt powerless, to stop the forces that were driving the destruction of the forest and the displacement of its inhabitants, including the Teak Tree. Ade really wanted to help his friend, but he understood that he couldn't do much to alter, what was going to happen. He also had a hidden anger towards the people who took away the Teak Tree. He couldn't understand why some people didn't appreciate how amazing nature is and why they would choose money and advancement over it.

The woodcutters walked up to the fallen giant tree. The woodcutters carefully began their work, breaking down the fallen giant piece by piece until only a scattered pile of wood remained. Ade, unaware of what was happening, stayed in the village and continued with his daily chores. Meanwhile, the fallen Teak Tree was placed onto a cart and covered with a tarpaulin to hide it from view. The cart, much smaller in comparison to the massive tree, began its journey towards the busy city of Imphal. Even though the wheels of the cart were making noise because of the weight, it still managed to move along the twisty paths.

The cart moved slowly and steadily through busy streets and crowded market places. People were too busy with their daily lives to notice it, unaware of the historical significance it carried. When the sun went down and the shadows got longer on the cobblestone streets, the cart at last made it to its destination - the busy center of Imphal, where business was booming with its own special beat. Ade would never learn about the destiny of the fallen Teak Tree; its remembrance would remain in his heart. In the busy city of Imphal, the fallen Teak Tree's journey came to an end at a large lumberyard on the outskirts. The Teak tree's destiny would be decided amidst the loud sounds of factories and machines. The massive Teak tree was unloaded from the cart, standing out against the bustling cityscape. When the cart stopped, a lot of things happened around it. The air smelled like fresh wood and sawdust. Workers in protective gear worked quickly and smoothly. The fallen Teak Tree stood quietly, its branches now just a pile of wood waiting to be used. The workers carefully began their tasks, skillfully shaping raw materials into various forms. Saws buzzed and hammers pounded in the bustling lumberyard, where each worker contributed to the intricate process of creation and destruction. Under the sun's gentle light, the fallen Teak Tree observed the unyielding march of progress, influenced by the hands of those determined to control nature.

Ade was unaware of what happened to the Teak Tree he considered a friend. The Teak Tree was measured, cut, and turned into various objects. Some became beams for buildings, others sculpture for the wealthy, and some were made into paper, becoming a part of society's fabric. As the hours turned into days and the days into weeks, the lumberyard was buzzing with activity, as the workers worked non-stop to keep up with the needs of the expanding city. The Teak Tree transformed into various shapes.

As Ade went about his everyday tasks in the calm Thangmeiband Village, he had no clue about the important things happening beyond its borders. But he cherished the memory of the Teak Tree.

Deep within the lumberyard, out of Ade's sight, the Teak Tree was turned from a grand forest giant into different furniture items for homes and businesses in the city. Skilled workers and carpenters worked really hard to make the wood, using their talented hands and their deep love for their craft... As Ade went about his daily routine in the village, the wood from the Teak Tree was skillfully crafted into tables, chairs, and cabinets. Each piece showcased the natural beauty and adaptability of the wood. Ade had no idea what was happening while they stayed in the village.

As Ade finished his everyday tasks in the village, he couldn't help but feel a growing sense of worry in his thoughts. He really missed the Teak Tree a lot, like a piece of himself went away with it. Ade didn't know that the tree had been taken to the city and turned into furniture. But he had a strange feeling that something wasn't right. Ade was determined to continue living in the village, despite feeling uneasy. He worked hard on his chores, thinking about the Teak Tree and the memories they had. Little did he know, his dear friend was far away. Its wood was being used for something new in the bustling city.

During peaceful moments of being alone, Ade was reminded of the Teak Tree. As he worked, he could hear the gentle rustling of leaves and the soft murmurs of the wind. Memories of the towering tree filled his mind, a symbol of hope in a world full of uncertainty. He remembered the hours spent with the tree, having whispered conversations beneath its leafy shelter. The bond they shared created a deep connection and a tapestry of shared experiences. Without the comforting shade of the Teak Tree, Ade felt lost, like a part of him was missing, creating a void that he couldn't fill. The familiar scenery of Thangmeiband Village appeared less vibrant without the grand tree that used to be its focal point.

In the midst of sorrow and doubt, Ade held onto the hope of reuniting with his dear friend and restoring their bond. He took comfort in the idea that the spirit of the Teak Tree continued to exist, intertwined with nature as a silent protector. As time went by, Ade carried on with his life, feeling the weight of missing something. But he believed that one day he would meet the Teak Tree again. He cherished the tree's wisdom and constant companionship, eagerly awaiting the moment to bask in its comforting shade again.

Although the Teak Tree's physical appearance may have disappeared due to time and progress, its memory remains in Ade's soul. It served as a guiding light during difficult times, reminding him of the everlasting strength of love and friendship in a world often filled with division and conflict.

And as he looked to the horizon with renewed determination, Ade vowed to honor the memory of the Teak Tree, not with tears of sorrow, but with acts of kindness and compassion, knowing that in doing so, he would keep alive the spirit of his beloved friend for generations to come.

The majestic teak tree's demise brought about a deep feeling of sorrow and grief as it was cut down and transformed into furniture. Each time the carpenter used his tools, it was like the tree was losing a piece of itself, leaving behind a feeling of emptiness and sorrow. The Teak Tree had been a quiet guardian in the Cheirou Ching woodland for many years, with its roots firmly planted in the rich soil and its branches stretching towards the sky. It has seen the years go by, life come and go, and had become a vital component of the forest's intricate balance.

However, after being turned into furniture, the tree couldn't help but feel a deep sense of sadness and detachment from its environment. It had always provided shelter and food for the forest animals, and represented strength and resilience in difficult times. But now, it was just seen as a product, its majestic shape reduced to mere objects that humans wanted.

As the furniture was being made, the tree couldn't help but feel sad about losing its old self. It missed the days when its branches would sway in the breeze, its leaves would whisper secrets to the wind, and its roots would draw nourishment from the soil. All that was left now, were memories of a time when the forest was full of life. Despite the sadness and hopelessness, the tree held onto a small ray of hope. Maybe, in its transformed state, it could still have a meaningful role, although different from before. Maybe, as a furniture piece, it could bring happiness and solace to its owners, reminding them of the splendor and grandeur of the original natural world it originated from. Despite the pain and sadness, the Teak Tree found a spark of hope. It realized that becoming furniture wasn't the end, but a fresh start. Even though it wouldn't be in the forest or home to animals anymore, the tree knew its wood would continue to exist in the city, bringing happiness to people.

It understood that its transformation into furniture meant that it would continue to serve a meaningful role in the lives of humans, bringing beauty and functionality to their homes and spaces.

When the tree got chopped and its wood was made into different furniture, it believed that its spirit would stay alive in every piece. It would bring happiness and coziness to the people who used them. The Teak Tree felt calm and happy, knowing that its story would continue, even if it turned out differently than it had expected. The Teak Tree bravely embraced its destiny with a newfound determination, thankful for the chance to keep spreading positivity and making a difference in the world. The teak tree's spirit continued to live on, forever connected to the people who were made happy, by the wood finding new homes. The Teak Tree felt a deep sense of acceptance as the finishing touches were gently added to the furniture made from its wood. The tree couldn't stay strong in the forest like before or be as grand as it used to be, but it felt better knowing that its memory would never fade.

The Teak Tree realized that as furniture, it had transformed into something more than just a tree. Its wood, crafted by expert hands, would now represent the lasting beauty and strength of nature, showing how all living things are connected. When the furniture finally settled into place, the Teak Tree felt happy and satisfied, realizing it had left a meaningful mark on anyone who saw it. Even if the tree's branches stopped moving and didn't share secrets anymore, its spirit would still live on in the hearts and thoughts of those who appreciated its beauty.

The Teak Tree's transition from a towering forest giant to simple furniture was not about losing, but about changing and starting anew. Even though it got smaller, it still stayed strong and full of life, connected to everything around it.

Chapter - 4

Life in Imphal City

In the peaceful village of Thangmeiband, calmness prevailed, surrounding its residents with a sense of simplicity and tranquility. In this beautiful Cheirou Ching forest, Ade, a curious and ambitious young boy, considered this perfect place his home. Living with him were his beloved family members - his hardworking father, Mr. Jackson, whose hands were rough from farming; his mother, Thoinu, whose kind-hearted nature brought warmth to their humble home; and his brother, Ryan, a symbol of youthful vitality and purity.

Ade and his family lived in sync with nature's rhythms. Every morning, they were greeted by the sweet melodies of birds and the gentle rustling of leaves. The forest was not just a backdrop for them, but the core of their livelihood. Mr. Jackson worked diligently in the lush greenery and towering trees, cultivating the land with unwavering dedication. From sunrise to sunset, he toiled under the warm sun, nurturing the earth to produce its abundant treasures.

The forest was a source of both nourishment and comfort in Ade's family's life. It provided them with fruits, vegetables, and grains to sustain their bodies and hearts. However, the Cheirou Ching forest was more than just a practical resource. It was a sanctuary for the soul, where dreams soared amidst the gentle rustling of leaves and the play of sunlight. Ade saw the forest as more than just a background to his everyday life; it was a place full of endless adventures and new discoveries. He loved chasing butterflies and climbing ancient trees, finding joy in the wonders of nature. The forest sparked his imagination and filled his heart with dreams and possibilities.

In the peaceful village, rumors of change floated in the air, brought by the gentle breeze in Cheirou Ching forest. As the world changed outside their village, new challenges arose, putting Ade's family and their beloved forest home at risk. The shadows of modernity crept closer, uncertain of what the future held. They confronted the challenges and difficulties that awaited them as a united front, finding courage in the enduring resilience that had been passed down through their family for many years. Over the years, a big, scary cloud appeared above the village, making everyone in the peaceful community feel unsure and worried. The noise of tools cutting through trees filled the air, showing the continuous destruction of the forest. Every tree that was cut down felt like a blow to the village, showing how the desire for advancement was endangering their way of life. As the days went by, the burden of adversity grew stronger, gradually draining Ade's family of their limited resources. The once lush and abundant forest, which had once provided them with sustenance and shelter, now stood as a stark reminder of human greed and its devastating consequences. Mr. Jackson worked really hard in the fields, his face full of worry and tiredness as he saw the land getting drier and producing less and less crops every season.

Thoinu, the pillar of strength in the family, did her best to shield her loved ones from the harsh realities of their changing world. However, even her unwavering determination started to falter, when confronted with such immense challenges. And Ade's brother Ryan used to be full of life and energy, but now he looked really scared as he saw the forest that he loved being destroyed. It used to be his safe haven from where he got his ideas. The burden of their situation weighed heavily on them, endangering their aspirations and ambitions, while they fought to endure in a world that appeared to be falling apart.

Amidst the deep sadness and emptiness, Ade stood out as a symbol of strong determination and perseverance. He didn't give in to the overwhelming feeling of despair that surrounded him. Instead, he found a powerful resolve within himself that shone brightly, bringing light to the darkness that loomed over his home. Ade didn't just see the forest as a bunch of trees. It was like a living thing, full of life and energy that never seemed to run out. It provided nourishment not only for his body but also for his soul, with its inherent beauty and peacefulness.

As Ade looked at the view in front of him, he felt a strong belief growing inside his heart. He understood that the path ahead would be full of danger and unknowns, with difficult challenges waiting at every corner. However, he also understood that he couldn't leave the land that had taken care of him since he was born, the land that had made him who he is today. As time went by, Ade became more determined, ready to face whatever obstacles came his way. The sun was setting, sending long shadows across the forest floor. Ade stood among the trees, looking ahead with an unwavering focus.

Ade promised himself and his homeland. He vowed to be a strong protector, a loyal defender of the forest's valuable heritage. Filled with strong determination, Ade began his adventure, prepared to face any obstacles in his mission to protect the purity and loveliness of his beloved land. Mr. Jackson and Thoinu faced fewer opportunities and many difficulties. They knew they had to make a tough choice. After thinking about it for a long time, they decided to leave their favorite village and start a new life in the busy city of Imphal. When Ade heard about his parents' decision to leave their village, he felt like a heavy weight pressing down on him. His heart felt heavy and sad, just like a rock sinking to the depths of a river. Ade's eyes filled with tears as he realized that they were going to leave soon.

Ade: "Mom, please stay in the village. I really don't want to go to the city."

Mom: "Ade, it's not safe for us here. Your father wants to leave the village because it's hard for us to find enough food."

Mom: "Ade, your brother Ryan also wants to concentrate on his studies. That's why we have to leave the village."

Ade: "Mom, I really love our village so much."

He knew that his family had to move to the busy city of Imphal for a better life. They believed that there were lots of chances and exciting things waiting for them... But, on the other hand, the thought of saying goodbye to everything he had always loved and treasured made him feel really upset and longing. Ade sat all by himself in his room, gazing out towards the forest with tears streaming down his face. He whispered, "I'm so sorry, my dear friend Teak Tree. I couldn't keep my promise to protect the forest. I'm just a kid, and I don't have any other choice but to leave the village for our future."

When Ade's heart was broken, everything around him seemed to get smaller and less colorful. The laughter of children playing in the streets and the gentle rustle of leaves in the wind suddenly disappeared, leaving a profound silence that seemed to bounce around in his head. Ade felt really confused and unsure about what was going on, he was struggling to accept it. He had a bunch of questions and worries in his mind. Would he ever be able to feel like he belonged in the new streets of Imphal? Would he be able to forget about his childhood memories and start fresh in a different place? Ade believed that the fresh path ahead would be full of obstacles and unknowns. With a sad heart and eyes full of tears, Ade said goodbye to the village that had been his home. He took with him the mixed feelings of happiness and sadness from the memories that he left behind. They were unsure and scared, but they believed it was the right choice to make their family's future better. The trip to Imphal was full of difficulties, every mile felt like a never-ending path of strangeness and difficulties. Ade's family, tired from the really long and hard trip, reached the busy city with a little bit of hope in their hearts and thoughts of a happier life swirling in their heads. When they entered the busy streets and lively markets of Imphal, they soon discovered that city life was much scarier than they thought it would be. The loud sounds all around them were too much to handle, making it hard for them to focus or relax. Everywhere they glanced, individuals were hurrying around, completely focused on their tasks, with determined expressions on their faces. The streets were filled with so much excitement and danger, every turn revealing a new and thrilling adventure. Ade's family, who had always resided in the quiet and serene Thangmeiband Village, discovered that the bustling and loud city life was a stark contrast to the peace and calm they were accustomed to. The roads were packed with people and it was really noisy. The air smelled like car smoke and there were so many people talking loudly. Everywhere they looked, there were huge buildings and busy markets, showing how much things have changed and improved. As Ade's family explored the new streets of Imphal, they faced lots of difficulties and problems. Ade's family had a really hard time finding a good place to live in Imphal. It was so difficult and they felt really frustrated and disappointed, every time they tried to look for some accomodation. In Thangmeiband Village, they resided in a simple but cozy house, surrounded by the lush greenery of nature's hug. But, in the busy city of Imphal, the situation with housing was completely opposite. There were way more people looking for a place to stay than places available, and the price to rent or buy a house was extremely expensive. Ade's family quickly realized that it wouldn't be easy to find a place which they could call their own, in this big city.

They searched all over the city, looking through ads, visiting many apartments and houses to find the right one. After looking at the apartments that were either too small, too old, or too expensive for their small budget, they felt really down and defeated. Ade's family had been searching for weeks, but unfortunately, they couldn't find any apartment within their budget. It was a tough reality for them to face, not being able to find the right place. They had exhausted all their options and ultimately decided to settle for a cozy apartment located on the outskirts of the city. The cost of renting an apartment within the city limits was simply too high for them to afford. They were unhappy with their new place. The new apartment was in a noisy area. They had no choice but to live in a small house.

Even though they had to face many difficulties, Ade's family never gave up and always tried their best to enjoy their new life in Imphal. They found comfort in the strong connections of love and unity that tied them together, seeking peace in the company of one another while exploring the unknown surroundings of their new house. They understand that the path ahead will be tough and full of obstacles, but they never gave up. They had faith that tomorrow will bring better opportunities and a chance to start anew. But adapting to the busy city lifestyle was a completely different challenge. The crowded streets, the constant noise, and the fast-paced lifestyle were overwhelming for Ade's family. Basic things like buying groceries or figuring out how to use the bus became really hard, and they felt confused and out of place in their new environment. They quickly understood that getting a job would be a difficult obstacle they needed to conquer. Mr. Jackson was a farmer who worked in the village of Thangmeiband. His skills were well-suited to the rhythms of village life, where agriculture was the primary source of livelihood for many families like theirs.

However, in the bustling city of Imphal, Mr. Jackson's expertise as a farmer proved to be of little use. The urban landscape offered few opportunities for agricultural work, and the skills that had served him well in the village were rendered obsolete, in this new environment. Mr. Jackson had to find a different job to help his family because he didn't have many choices. Ade's family worked really hard, but they didn't earn enough money to cover all their expenses. They were constantly worried about how they would be able to afford everything. Even though they had to face many difficulties, Ade's family never lost hope. They drew strength from each other, supporting one another through the ups and downs of their new life in the city. They thought about why they chose to move - wanting a better future, looking forward to new chances, and dreaming of a life they could feel good about.

Living in Imphal was completely different from the peacefulness of Thangmeiband village. Ade's family used to enjoy the peaceful life in the countryside, but now they are surrounded with the busy city life. The change was really hard at first, but as time went on, they started feeling more comfortable in their new place.

In the busy town of Imphal, Mr. Jackson, Ade's father, had managed to secure steady employment as a construction worker. Every day, he worked hard in the hot sun, his hands rough and his forehead sweaty as he tirelessly built the tall buildings in the city. Even though his job was really tough and being away from his family often, Mr. Jackson always worked hard and made sure that his loved ones are looked after nicely.

Meanwhile, Thoinu, Ade's mother, took on various odd jobs to help the family's income and make ends meet. She dedicated herself to various tasks, from tidying up homes and doing dishes to peddling homemade items at the nearby market, all in order to provide for her family's necessities and give her children the best opportunities to succeed. Despite the difficulties she encountered and the tiredness that frequently loomed over her, Thoinu tackled every task with elegance and determination. Her unwavering determination acted as a source of strength and motivation for her family.

Together, Mr. Jackson and Thoinu worked hand in hand, their efforts fueled by a shared desire to build a better future for themselves and their children. Even though they had to work for a long time, earn very little money, and face many challenges, they never gave up on their promise to help Ade and his brother achieve their goals. They tried their best, to hide the challenges they had in earning money from their kids.

Their sacrifices were not in vain, as they knew that their hard work and determination would eventually lead to success, creating a better future for their loved ones.

As months turned into years, the resilience and perseverance of Ade's family began to yield fruit. They worked really hard and never gave up. Finally, they managed to save up a lot of money. They used the money to start their very own grocery store in the busy city center. The Ade Family Store's story is all about never giving up, working really hard, and chasing a big dream. This dream is not just about making money, but also about owning a home.

The Ade Family Store began like many other small businesses—a humble beginning marked by long hours, tight budgets, and uncertain prospects. Ade's parents worked really hard on the store, using all their money and even borrowing from people they knew to keep it running. Their adventure was full of obstacles; bigger stores trying to outdo them, market changes that kept going up and down, and not knowing what would happen with the economy, made them question their determination. However, the Ade parents never gave up, driven by their strong dedication to their community and their hope for a brighter future for their family.

The Ade Family Store was special not just because their products were great and affordable, but because they always made sure every customer felt important. Customers were more than just sales, they were like neighbors, buddies, and part of the family. Ade and his family were proud to remember their customers' names, predict what they needed, and do more than expected to make sure they were happy. The idea of truly caring and connecting with others helped build a strong foundation of loyalty and trust, which was a key to their achievements. The Ade Family Store became really popular in the community because everyone heard about how nice they were and how great their service was. Now it was a time when, the small store in the neighborhood turned into a cherished place for everyone—a spot where people not only went to buy things but also to chat about what's happening, exchange tales, and ask for guidance.

The store turned into a real important place for the community, where they held events, helped out with local projects, and ultimately became a spot where people could come together and support each other. The Ade Family Store was doing great and thus they started dreaming even bigger because they were becoming more and more successful. There was a time, when the Ade family faced difficulties in earning sufficient money. But now, they were brave enough to dream about having their very own house. It would be a unique place where they can build a promising future for themselves and their children. A safe haven filled with stability and security awaited them.

They were really focused on making their dream come true, so they started to plan out their finances and save money every month to buy a house. Ade's parents made a lot of sacrifices to buy a house. They had to give up many things to make it happen. Ade's parents saved money, gave up fancy things, and made smart choices about money, all to make a better life for their family.

After many years of working hard and giving up things, the big day came—the Ade family finally owned their own home. They understood that their achievements were not only because of their hard work, but also because of the kindness and encouragement from their community.

The community had warmly welcomed their store and played a significant role in making their dreams come true. Today, the Ade Family Store is still doing really well, not just as a successful business but also as a sign of hope and motivation for the people in the area.

The Ade family, who are now proud owners of a house, are still dedicated to helping their community, supporting local projects, and sharing the good things that have come their way. Their adventure is a reminder that if you keep trying, stay focused, and believe in yourself, dreams can really come true. Even the biggest dreams, like having your own house, is be possible if you work hard.

Everyone in the neighborhood knew about their store. Over some time, their sales reached an all-time high. They stocked everything needed for daily household chores. They were brave enough to take a big risk, even though it was dangerous. They were prepared to chase their goal of being financially secure and self-sufficient.

Ade was so happy and proud when he saw how his family went from having a hard time to emerge as winners... It made him feel really responsible and proud to see them doing so well. As he grew older and became a young man, he started to feel a strong urge to help his family succeed and ease some of the weight off his parents' shoulders. Despite being young, Ade understood the challenges of saving money and he was grateful for the sacrifices, his parents made to look after him and his brother. He grabbed every chance to make money, working part-time after finishing college and on weekends to help add to the family's income.

Ade was very excited and proud because he was able to improve his family's financial situation by working a part-time job. He was happy that he could help his family in a big way and was thankful for the chances he had to do so. Ade worked really hard and never gave up. He made their grocery store stronger and brought his family closer, as they all worked towards a better future.

After years of hard work and perseverance, Ade's family had finally achieved their dream of homeownership. After a lot of effort and never giving up, Ade's family finally made their dream come true and bought a house. One day, Ade's dad saw an ad in the newspaper, about a house that was up for sale. He was really excited and talked to his wife, Thoinu, about it. They both decided to go and see the house. Ade's dad dialed the number in the ad and a guy named Rocky picked up the phone and said, "Hello."

Jackson: "Hi, I saw your ad in the newspaper. Are you selling a house?"

Rocky: "Yes, I am."

Jackson: "Can you let me know where it is?"

Rocky: "I'll give you the address before you come to see it."

Jackson: "I'll try to come tomorrow."

Rocky: "Alright, I'll send you the address to your phone."

Jackson: "How much are you asking for the house?"

Rocky: "I'm asking for Rs.75,0000."

Jackson: "That's a bit steep. Can we negotiate on the price?"

Rocky: "I'm willing to negotiate, but not too much. Let's discuss it when you come and see the house."

Jackson: "Alright, I'll see you tomorrow then. Thank you."

Rocky: "Looking forward to meeting you. See you tomorrow."

The next day, Jackson couldn't wait to go to Rocky's house. He was so excited and couldn't stop thinking about it. As he approached the front door, he couldn't help but feel a sense of nervousness. This meeting would determine whether his dreams of owning a property would finally come true.

Rocky greeted Jackson with a warm smile, inviting him inside. They settled down in the cozy living room, surrounded by the comforting scent of freshly brewed coffee. The two got engaged in a lively conversation, knowing each other's lives before diving into the topic at hand.

Jackson brought up the topic of the cost in a very serious way. He had done his research, meticulously analyzing the market value of similar properties in the area. He presented his findings to Rocky, who listened attentively, nodding in agreement at the figures Jackson had quoted.

After a thorough discussion, Jackson and Rocky finally reached a mutual agreement, on the amount they would consider for the property. It was a fair price that satisfied both parties, taking into account the property's condition, location, and potential for future development.

Feeling a sense of relief and accomplishment, Jackson and Rocky moved on to the next crucial step – setting a date for payment and the official transfer of ownership. They meticulously went through the legalities, ensuring that all the necessary paperwork and documentation would be done in order. It was unbelievable that that they had bought Mr. Rocky's house. Ade's family was so lucky, when they found an incredible chance to make their dream of owning a home a reality. It seemed like a once-in-a-lifetime opportunity that was almost too good to be true!

As they stepped through the front door, Ade's family couldn't help but feel a sense of awe and wonder at the sight before them. The house was everything they had ever hoped for and more - spacious rooms bathed in natural light, a cozy fireplace for chilly evenings, and a lush garden brimming with vibrant blooms. It was a far cry from the cramped confines of their apartment, where space had always been a luxury that they couldn't afford.

For Ade's parents, the opportunity to purchase Mr. Rocky's house was more than just a chance to upgrade their living condition - it was a symbol of their hard work and their perseverance finally paying off. After years of struggle and sacrifice, they finally had the opportunity to provide their family a comfortable and a secure home where they could build lasting memories together.

With hearts full of excitement and anticipation, Ade's family wasted no time in making an offer on the house. They knew that such opportunities were rare and that they couldn't afford to let this one slip through their fingers. As they signed the paperwork and finalized the deal, a sense of relief washed over them, knowing that they were one step closer to achieving their long-held dream of home ownership. As Ade's family settled into their new house, they couldn't help but feel an overwhelming sense of thankfulness for the surprising chain of events, that led them here. They were aware of their good fortune in being able to purchase such a house, and they made a promise to treasure and maintain it for many years.

Before going to sleep, they discussed the unexpected events that brought them to their new home, while sitting in the peaceful living room. They were aware that their adventure was not yet finished and that obstacles would surely come their way. But at that moment, they enjoyed the warmth and comfort of their new home, feeling thankful, for the chance to begin afresh and create a better future.

Ade's family was amazed by the beauty and grace of their new home, as they went around exploring it. Every corner of the house, from the big living room to the comfy bedrooms, was completely content. Ade was fascinated by the furniture because each piece was so nicely crafted and looked special. The fancy furniture in the rooms caught his attention right away. Each piece seemed to tell a story, its intricate carvings and elegant lines a testament to the skill and craftsmanship of its creator.

Ade was completely fascinated by one particular item - a beautiful cabinet made with great skill from teak wood. The cabinet looked really nice in the living room, with its shiny surfaces and fancy designs standing out against the rough tree bark outside. Ade couldn't stop staring at the beautiful wood with its amazing golden colors. It was so captivating that he couldn't keep his eyes away.

As he ran his fingers along the smooth surface of the cabinet, Ade couldn't help but feel a sense of connection to the tree, from which it had come. He imagined the teak tree standing tall and majestic in the heart of the forest, its branches reaching for the sky and its roots sinking deep into the earth. He wondered about the journey the tree had taken, from the tranquility of the forest to the bustling city, and the transformation it had undergone along the way.

Ade suddenly felt a strong desire to discover more about the tree, that had turned into his family's furniture. He looked for books and articles about woodworking and forestry, excited to learn about the mysteries of the teak tree and the skill that made it into something so beautiful. His interest kept growing as he made more discoveries, and he felt himself getting more and more involved in the art of making furniture and designing.

As Ade delved deeper into his newfound passion for furniture, he himself began to experiment with woodworking, using scraps of wood and discarded materials to create his own pieces of art. At first, his creations were simple and rough around the edges, but with time and practice, he honed his skills and developed a unique style of his own.

His family watched with pride as Ade's talent blossomed, his creations earning praise and admiration from friends and neighbors. They encouraged him to pursue his passion further, enrolling him in woodworking classes and providing him with the tools and resources he needed to succeed. For Ade, woodworking became more than just a hobby - it was a form of expression, a way to connect with the world around him and leave his mark on the world. With each piece he created, he poured his heart and soul into his work, infusing it with the same sense of wonder and fascination, that had captivated him from the very beginning.

And as he looked to the future, Ade knew that his journey was just beginning. With his family's support and encouragement, he embarked on a new chapter in his life, one filled with endless possibilities and boundless creativity. And though he didn't know what the future held, he knew that as long as he had his passion for woodworking, he could accomplish anything that he would set his mind to.

Ade's life journey took an unexpected turn when he embarked on a journey into the world of furniture-making. Born and raised in the serene village of Thangmeiband, Ade had led a simple life, surrounded by the beauty of nature and the love of his family. But everything changed when he discovered his passion for woodworking and embarked on a journey, that would shape the course of his life forever.

Growing up in Thangmeiband, Ade had always been drawn to the natural world around him. He spent his days exploring the forest, climbing trees, and marveling at the wonders of the world around him. But it wasn't until he stumbled upon a woodworking workshop in the nearby town, that he discovered his true passion. While Ade observed the artisans creating beautiful furniture out of wood, he felt a burst of inspiration inside him. He was completely fascinated, how beautiful and well-made their creations were. Right then and there, he realized that he wanted to know everything about woodworking and become a skilled craftsman just like them. With determination and a thirst for knowledge, Ade began to immerse himself in the world of woodworking. He spent hours studying books and articles on woodworking techniques, learning about different types of wood and the tools used to shape them. He practiced his skills whenever he could, carving small pieces of wood into intricate designs and experimenting with different techniques.

As Ade's passion for woodworking grew, he sought out mentors who could help him hone his skills and develop his craft. One such mentor was Mr. Patel, a seasoned woodworker who had been crafting furniture for decades. Mr. Patel took Ade under his wing, teaching him the finer points of woodworking and instilling in him a sense of discipline and dedication to his craft.

Under Mr. Patel's guidance, Ade's skills flourished. He learned how to select the perfect piece of wood for each project, how to use hand tools and power tools with precision, and how to bring his creative visions to life through his work. But more than that, he learned the value of patience and perseverance, as he spent hours perfecting his craft and striving to create pieces of beauty and elegance.

With Mr. Patel's guidance and support, Ade began to create his own masterpieces. From elegant tables and chairs to intricate cabinets and chests, Ade poured his heart and soul into each piece, infusing them with his own unique style and creativity. His work garnered praise and admiration from all who saw it, and soon, he found himself gaining recognition as a talented and skilled craftsman.

But for Ade, woodworking was more than just a means of earning a living - it was a form of expression, a way to connect with the world around him and leave his mark on the world. He poured his heart and soul into his work, drawing inspiration from the beauty of nature and the rich cultural heritage of his homeland. And with each piece he created, he felt a sense of fulfillment and purpose unlike anything, he had ever experienced before.

As Ade's reputation as a master craftsman grew, so too did his impact on the world around him. His furniture was highly desired by collectors and fans alike, and people were willing to pay a lot of money for it. The rich and powerful even decorated their homes with his pieces. But not only that, Ade's adventure motivated other people to chase their own interests and pursue their dreams, even if they appeared to be extremely difficult.

Ade's transformation from a regular boy to a skilled craftsman was a really long and tough journey. It had lots of good times and bad times, moments of success and moments of failure. When Ade thought about his journey, he felt really proud and thankful for everything that he had achieved. He knew that his life has changed forever by his love of woodworking, and he was grateful, for the opportunity to share his passion with the world. And as he continued to create beautiful pieces of furniture, Ade knew that his journey was far from over, and that the best was yet to come.

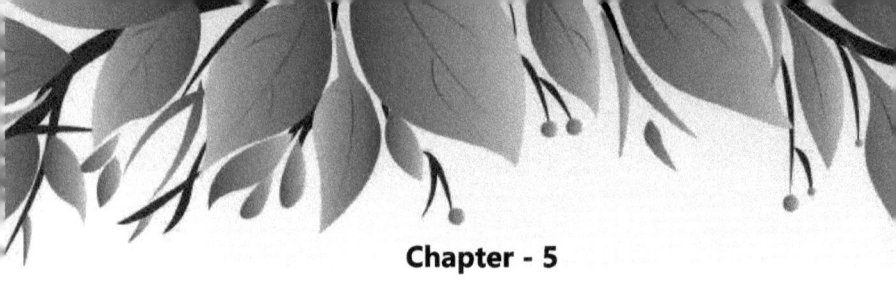

Chapter - 5

The Mysterious Neighbours

Ade's family had just moved to a calm and quiet neighborhood, and it felt like they were living in a wonderful dream. The busy city of Imphal gave them a brand-new beginning, completely different from the challenges that they had experienced in their previous village. From the moment they arrived, Ade's family was welcomed with kindness and friendliness by their new neighbors. They were welcomed into the community with open arms, and Ade felt a sense of belonging beginning to bloom within him. The kindness and generosity of their neighbors made them feel right at home, and Ade knew that they had made the right decision in choosing to move to Imphal.

As Ade began to explore his new surroundings, he discovered a world of wonder and excitement waiting right outside his doorstep. He walked down the curvy streets, enjoying the colorful houses, the bustling markets, and the pretty green parks all over the place. Everywhere he looked, there was something new and exciting to discover, and Ade felt his sense of connection to his new home growing stronger with each passing day.

As the days turned into weeks, Ade and his family settled into a comfortable routine in their new home. They unpacked their belongings, decorated their rooms, and made the house their own. Ade relished the simple pleasures of everyday life – the smell of his mother's cooking wafting through the air, the sound of laughter echoing through the halls, and the warmth of his family's love surrounding him at every turn. One of the things that made Ade feel most at home in Imphal was the friendships he formed with the other friends in the neighborhood. They welcomed him with open arms, inviting him to join in their games and adventures. Ade felt a sense of camaraderie and belonging among his new friends, and he cherished the bonds of friendship that they shared.

Imphal was a city rich in culture and tradition, and Ade was eager to immerse himself in everything it had to offer. He attended festivals and celebrations, sampled local delicacies, and learned about the history and customs of the people who called Imphal their home. With each new experience, Ade felt a deeper connection to the city and its people, and he knew that he was beginning to truly belong. As Ade navigated the ups and downs of life in Imphal, he found comfort in the familiar routines and rituals of everyday life. He savored the simple pleasures of a home-cooked meal, a quiet evening spent reading by the fire, and a leisurely stroll through the neighborhood with his family. These little moments of coziness and familiarity made Ade feel connected to his new home, reminding him that he was in the right place. One of the things that made Ade feel most at home in Imphal was the strong sense of community that permeated the city. When a neighbor needed help or there was a reason to celebrate, the folks in Imphal always had each other's backs. They stuck together through good times and bad. They stayed united through both happy and tough times. Ade felt a sense of belonging among his fellow citizens, and he knew that he was a valued member of the community.

As Ade settled into life in Imphal, he began to put down roots in his new home. He invested time and energy into the community, volunteering his talents to help those in need and participating in local events and initiatives. In doing so, Ade forged deep and meaningful connections with the people around him, and he felt a profound sense of belonging that filled him with pride and joy. As Ade reflected on his journey, he realized that home wasn't just a place – it was a feeling, a sense of belonging that came from the heart. Imphal had become more than just a city to Ade – it was his home, a place where he felt loved, accepted, and valued. And as he looked to the future, Ade knew that no matter where life took him, Imphal would always be the place, where he belonged.

But their tranquility was short-lived, shattered by the arrival of a new family who moved in next door. When they first came, there was a sense of secrecy and doubt surrounding them, making the once-calm neighborhood feel uneasy. As Ade's family observed their new neighbors from a distance, they couldn't help but feel a sense of unease creeping over them. The family seemed a little strange, but they couldn't figure out exactly what it was. Rumors began to circulate among the other residents, whispers of strange happenings and peculiar behavior only added to the sense of foreboding that hung in the air.

Despite their best efforts to ignore the rumors and go about their daily lives, Ade's family couldn't shake the feeling that something wasn't right. They were always on high alert, carefully observing their new neighbors, closely monitoring their actions with increasing doubt and worry. A gloomy shadow seemed to cover the cheerful neighborhood, bringing sadness to their recent joy and putting their hard-earned peace at risk.

The Sharma family enjoyed spending time with each other and hardly ever went out of their house except for occasional tasks. They were happy being alone, finding comfort in the coziness of their house. Their conversations with others were always nice and friendly, but there was something about the way they acted that made people feel uncomfortable, whenever they were around. Ade's family, being new to the neighborhood, had a friendly introduction with the Sharmas. They exchanged pleasantries and engaged in small talks, but there was always an underlying tension that lingered in the air. It seemed like the Sharmas had a hidden secret, something they didn't want to tell anyone outside their family.

Their conversations were brief and guarded, leaving Ade's family with a sense of curiosity mixed with unease. The Sharmas seemed to have a knack for diverting any personal questions, skillfully changing the subject whenever someone delved too deep into their lives. This evasiveness only added to the discomfort that surrounded them. As time went on, the unease grew stronger. The Sharmas rarely attended community events or social gatherings, further isolating themselves from the neighborhood. Everyone noticed that they weren't there, and people started whispering to each other about the strange couple who lived next door. The Sharmas' strange behavior always made the air feel weird whenever they were nearby. Their presence alone was enough to make others feel on edge, as if they were constantly being watched or judged. Despite their unsettling nature, the Sharmas never displayed, any overtly malicious behavior. They were simply enigmatic, keeping their distance from the outside world and maintaining an air of secrecy. This left Ade's family and the rest of the neighborhood with a lingering sense of discomfort, a feeling that something was amiss, but could never quite be pinpointed.

Ade and his brother Ryan were in the yard one evening, when they saw something unusual happening next door. A delivery truck arrived at the Sharma's house, and the driver started unloading crates of goods with a secretive demeanor. Ade became curious and observed closely from behind the fence, wanting to unravel the mystery surrounding his neighbors' actions.

As Ade and Ryan watched, they noticed that the crates being unloaded were labeled with a foreign language, they couldn't quite make out. The driver looked like he was rushing, quickly looking around with a nervous expression on his face. Ade's curiosity was piqued even further as he wondered, what could be inside those mysterious crates. Mrs. Sharma came out of the house and started helping the driver unload the crates. Ade could see the excitement on her face, and he couldn't help but wonder, what was so special about the contents of those crates.

As the last crate was unloaded, Ade saw Mrs. Sharma hand the driver a wad of cash, and he quickly got into the truck and drove off. Ade turned to Ryan, his eyes wide with excitement, and whispered, "We need to find out what's in those crates. "The following day, Ade and Ryan chose to investigate. They waited for the Sharma family to depart. They were curious about the contents of the crate. However, the Sharma family never left the house; they always stayed inside. Ade and Ryan decided to take the matter into their own hands and approached the Sharma family's house. They tapped on the door, but nobody replied. They could hear muffled voices coming from inside, but no one came to the door.

Determined to uncover the mystery of the crate, Ade and Ryan decided to wait outside the house. They watched as the Sharma family moved around inside, never once stepping a foot outside. Hours passed, and still, there was no sign of them leaving. As the sun began to set, Ade and Ryan grew more anxious. They knew they had to act fast before the Sharma family caught on to their snooping. With a sense of urgency, they made a plan to sneak into the house under the cover of darkness. As they crept closer to the house, they could hear the Sharma family talking loudly. It was now or never. Ade and Ryan took a deep breath and made their move, slipping through an open window and into the house.

They found something inside that was even more incredible, than they could have ever imagined. The crate was filled with stacks of money, jewels, and other valuable items. It was clear that the Sharma family was involved in some sort of illegal activity. Before they could process what, they had discovered, they heard footsteps approaching. Panicked, Ade and Ryan quickly grabbed a few items from the crate and made a run, narrowly escaping before they were caught. As they made their way back home, Ade and Ryan knew they had stumbled upon something dangerous. But they also knew that they had to find a way to expose the Sharma family's illegal activities before it was too late. Ade knew they had to do something about it.

Ade and Ryan quickly informed the authorities about the evidence they found, leading to the arrest of the Sharmas... The evidence Ade and Ryan found was crucial in building a case against the Sharmas , who had been involved in a string of illegal activities for months. The police were able to track down the Sharma hideout and apprehend them before they could cause any more harm to the community. Ade and Ryan's fast decision-making and courage not only led to the Sharmas being caught, but also stopped more crimes from happening. Their actions were commended by the authorities, and they were hailed as heroes in their neighborhood.

The Sharmas were charged with multiple offenses, including theft, fraud, and drug trafficking. Thanks to Ade and Ryan's cooperation with the police, the Sharmas were convicted and sentenced to a lengthy prison term. The community breathed a sigh of relief knowing that the Sharmass were behind the bars and that Ade and Ryan had played a crucial role in bringing them to justice. Their actions served as a reminder that ordinary citizens can make a difference in fighting crime and keeping their neighborhoods safe. In the days that followed, life in the neighborhood returned to normal, with Ade and Ryan regaling their friends with tales of their daring adventure. The memory of their encounter with the mysterious neighbors would linger in their minds for years to come, a reminder of the importance of staying vigilant and standing up against injustice wherever it may be found. And as Ade looked out across the yard at the now-empty house next door, he felt a sense of pride knowing that he had played a part in uncovering the truth and bringing an end to the Sharma's reign of terror. With a newfound sense of confidence and determination, he knew that no mystery would ever be too great for him to solve.

Ade's new house, purchased from Mr. Rocky, is packed with furniture crafted from the Teak Tree. This furniture is very important to him and is linked to his dreams and feelings. It forms a powerful connection that accompanies him on his adventures. As a kid, Ade would play in the forest where the Teak Trees thrived. He sensed a deep bond between himself and the furniture in his room. As Ade got older, his affection for the Teak Tree and its furniture grew even stronger. He would a spend lot of time looking at the detailed work and the beautiful, cozy colors of the wood. Every item appeared to hold a tale, a past that connected with his own adventures.

The table in the dining room, was where his family ate together, making happy memories and telling stories. The chairs, old and worn, heard many talks and gave comfort. The bed, strong and cozy, gave him peace and safety when he couldn't sleep. But it wasn't only the furniture there that meant something to Ade. He also felt a special bond with the Teak Trees. He thought that the trees had a special kind of wisdom, a knowledge that lasted for a long time. Their strength and ability to bounce back from challenges were just like his own hopes and dreams. Ade felt comfort and motivation in his room, filled with beautiful Teak Tree furniture. It was like a safe place where he could escape from the busy world and explore his own ideas and feelings. The furniture seemed to connect him to his dreams, reminding him of the amazing life he wanted to have. As Ade started his adventure in life, the connection between him and the Teak Tree furniture stayed strong. Whether he was staying up late studying at his desk or relaxing with a book in his beloved armchair, the furniture always reminded him of where he came from and the aspirations he cherished.

Even though he faced many challenges and problems, having the Teak Tree furniture nearby always made him feel powerful and sure of himself. It reminded him of how the trees never backed down, staying tall and sturdy even during hard times. It turned into a sign of his own perseverance and the idea that he could conquer any obstacle that crossed his path. Throughout his life, Ade continued to cherish the Teak Tree furniture, passing it down through generations.

Each piece carried with it a piece of his story, a testament to his dreams and emotions. And as he looked back on his journey, he knew that the bond he shared with the furniture would forever be a part of him, a reminder of the power of connection and the beauty of dreams.

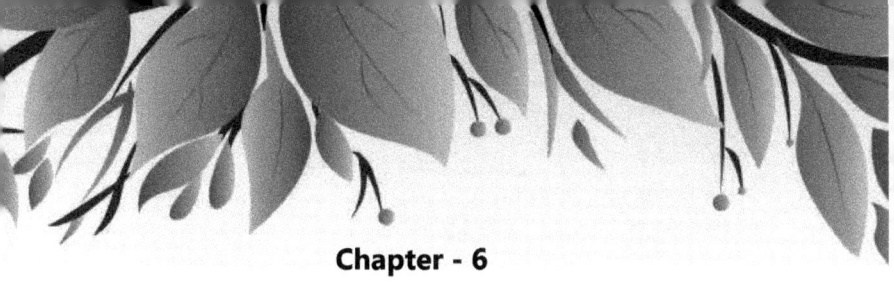

Chapter - 6

Dark Revelations

In the dark of night, Ade's family slept soundly, not knowing the danger that was just outside their door. Suddenly, a loud crash shattered the silence as the front door was forcefully kicked open, breaking the wooden frame. Ade's parents, Mr. Jackson and Thoinu, woke up in a panic, their hearts pounding with fear and confusion. Before they could understand what was happening, a mysterious figure appeared from the shadows, wearing a scary mask and giving off an evil vibe. In the dark room, Ade's scared eyes caught sight of a shiny gun as the intruder showed it with a scary look. The sound of the gun being prepared made them feel even more scared, a sign that something bad was about to happen.

Ade's dad, Mr. Jackson, quickly jumped in front of his family to protect them from danger. He felt a strong urge to keep them safe, especially when faced with a big danger. However, his brave attempts were useless against the heartless attacker who aimed their weapon with deadly accuracy. The room was filled with a really loud gunshot that echoed through the night. It felt like time stopped as the bullet hit its target, cutting through the air with a lot of power, heading straight for the peacefulness of the family. Thoinu let out a loud scream of pain when she saw her husband fall to the ground, blood spilling everywhere. Ryan, Ade's big brother, stayed close to his mom, crying and holding onto her tightly, looking absolutely terrified.

Ade couldn't move, he was so shocked and couldn't believe what he was seeing. His brain was trying really hard to understand the scary thing happening right in front of him. The wicked fellow, after finishing his evil plan, disappeared into the dark night, leaving behind a lot of sadness and destruction. After the scary experience, Ade's family was completely broken and scared, their calm life, forever changed by fate. The sounds of the attack lingered in their house, showing how fragile life can be and how darkness can be so scary.

Ade's family was really scared and sad as they hurriedly picked up the phone, trying hard to call the police station. Each time the phone rang, it felt like a plea for assistance, a light of hope during their difficult time. When Ade's mother, Thoinu, answered the call, her voice was full of emotion as she tried to explain the terrible thing that happened at home. She sounded so sad and scared, begging for help, like she was praying to the sky. At the other side of the phone, a peaceful and unwavering voice answered, comforting them that assistance was coming. Ade's family held onto those words like a guiding light in the midst of the darkness, their trust in the officials' shining through their sadness.

Suddenly, the loud wailing of sirens broke the silence of the night, getting louder with every second. When the police arrived, a feeling of comfort and safety washed over them, reminding them that they had someone to rely on in their moment of distress. As the police rushed into the house, their faces serious and determined, Ade's family told the terrifying story of what had happened. They spoke with so much emotion and desperation, like a flood of words pouring out. As they shared each detail, it felt like their pain was getting a little lighter. They were determined to find justice for their loved one, who had passed away.

After hearing about the terrible attack on Ade's family, the police didn't waste any time. They quickly started a big investigation to find out what happened. The police knew how serious the situation was, so they used all their skills and resources to figure out the truth about the awful crime, that had shocked everyone in the community. The start of the real police investigation was the beginning of a careful process to find out every single thing about the attack and figure out who did such a bold act of violence. They followed every possible clue with strong determination, as detectives and officers worked nonstop to understand what happened on that important night.

The detectives wanted to make sure the criminals faced the consequences of their actions. They searched every inch, examining the crime scene and interviewing witnesses who saw it all. As the investigation went on, a clearer picture started to come together, showing more about why the attack happened. With each clue found and every person interviewed, the mystery began to unravel, leading detectives closer to the truth every day.

The informant's tip about politicians, gangsters, and lenders being involved in the teak wood business made the investigation into the attack on Ade's family even more complicated. This shocking revelation surprised the police and made them worry about the possible role of important people in the crime. The police got a tip from someone that said, people connected to the teak wood industry might have planned the attack on Ade's family. The tip pointed fingers at politicians, gangsters, and lenders who were supposedly doing illegal stuff with teak wood. The surprising discovery made investigators more curious about the reasons for the attack, leading them to investigate further into the links between the attackers and the teak wood industry. The participation of politicians, criminals, and moneylenders brought up concerning issues about corruption, organized crime, and the misuse of natural resources for personal profit.

The tip from the informant helped the police a lot in their search for justice. It gave them a better idea of why the attack happened and how the people behind it might have done it. The tip also showed how serious the crime was, and how dangerous, illegal activities in the teak wood industry can be for the community's safety. When the investigators looked into the tip from the informant, they had a lot of problems to deal with. They had to figure out a complicated network of connections and unravel all the lies and trickery surrounding the teak wood business. It was even harder because important people with a stake in the industry were involved, making things even more confusing. The investigators never gave up though, as they tried their best to find out, what really happened in the attack.

Even though there were risks and dangers, the police were determined to seek justice for Ade's family and make sure the people who attacked them were held quickly... The tip from the informant was really important because it helped the police start their investigation and look into why the attack happened. They wanted to find out all the details about what happened and why.

After getting a tip from someone, the police started investigating about Solomon Singh, a gangster from Imphal who knew a lot of important people, like politicians and teak businessmen. When they found out about Solomon Singh, it made the police really worried. They were shocked by how much power he had and how many immoral things he was doing.

As the investigation progressed, law enforcement officials conducted further inquiries and gathered evidence linking Solomon Singh to the violent attack on Ade's family. They uncovered a web of connections between Solomon Singh, politicians, and teak businessmen, suggesting that the attack probably had been orchestrated, as part of a larger conspiracy involving organized crime and corruption.

Politicians, especially took advantage of their powerful positions to put pressure on the police and meddle with the investigation. They used their connections and resources to protect themselves and their friends from being investigated, which made it hard for the police to follow leads and collect evidence properly. Gangsters such as Solomon Singh, who had built up groups of loyal supporters and workers, were a big danger to the investigation. They used violence, threats, and fear to make witnesses stay quiet, stop justice from being served, and keep their illegal businesses safe.

The teak businessmen who were involved in the case also had a part in stopping and getting in the way of the investigation. They used their money and power to control the legal system, mess with the proof, and block the path of fairness, all to keep their illegal actions safe and avoid getting in trouble. It was a calm afternoon at Ade's house, the loud knock on the door made everyone in the family feel nervous, wondering who it could be. Ade's mom walked to the door carefully, looking worried. When she opened it, she saw a serious police officer staring back at her, making the room feel tense. The officer began speaking right away, his voice grave as he recounted the investigation. Ade's family paid close attention, feeling extremely upset and shocked by the information they were hearing about the challenges in seeking justice. The officer's words painted a grim and frightening picture of deceit and falsehoods, revealing the involvement of a politician and a teak wood businessman in the crime. While the officer was talking, Ade's mom, Thoinu, started feeling scared and infuriated, her hands shaking with strong feelings.

The police officer's words echoed loudly in their ears, like a serious command, reminding them of the hidden dangers. He told them to be watchful and stay away from the influential people involved in the investigation. He stressed on how crucial it was to stay safe when facing immediate danger. After the officer said goodbye and walked away, Ade's family had to face the tough truth of their new circumstances. The officer's words felt heavy and made their home feel gloomy. They started getting worried.

Ade's mom told Ade and Ryan that she was scared after hearing the police officer's warning. She wanted to move to a different place. Ade sat in his room, feeling heavy with worry. The thought of leaving his home made him feel sad and uncertain. As he looked around his room, his heart was filled with mixed emotions.

When Ade was feeling sad, he thought about the teak tree in the forest. As he glanced around, he noticed something incredible - the furniture in the room seemed to come alive! The chairs and tables were softly glowing, and Ade even felt them whispering to each other.

Ade was both confused and curious. He moved closer, trying to hear the soft whispers. To his surprise, the voices became louder and he could understand the words they were saying. It felt like the furniture had come alive, each piece having its own unique voice.

"Listen, Ade," one of the chairs whispered, its voice soft and soothing. "We have been here with you through it all, silently witnessing your joys and sorrows."

Another piece, a small side table, chimed in, its voice tinged with warmth. "You are not alone, Ade. We are here to support you, just as the Teak Tree once did."

Ade felt so many emotions in his heart, when he heard the kind words from his furniture. It was like they were telling him to be strong and never give up, even when things were tough.

Ade felt a wave of calmness come over him, as he shut his eyes and let the comforting atmosphere of his room surround him. At that instant, he understood that he could tackle all the obstacles that came his way, thanks to the encouragement of his faithful friends.

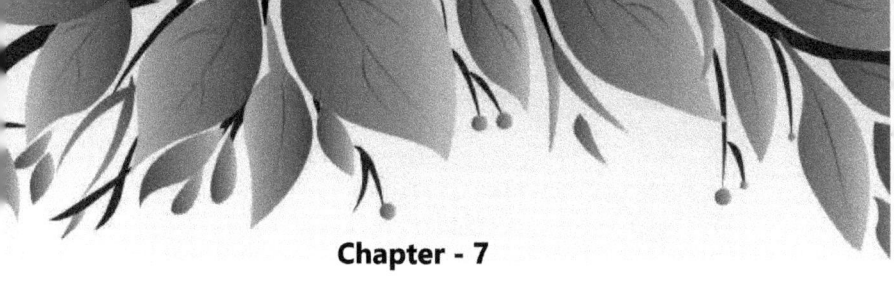

Chapter - 7

Recognizing the Need for Power

Ade understands that facing powerful individuals will be difficult, and he cannot face them by himself. He requires companions, assistance, and resources to have a fighting chance against those who have all the control. Ade understands that these people may have a lot of cash and people to help them. Ade knows he can't battle against them all by himself, so he's trying to gather his own gang of supporters. Ade knows that dealing with important people can be dangerous because they might try to get back at him. But if he gets help from others and makes friends, he can lower the risks and have a better chance of achieving his goals. By teaming up with people who want the same things as him, he can be stronger and safer against any dangers that might come his way.

Ade join the Like-Minded Political Party with the help of Dr. Sukhdev Singh. He really wants justice and accountability. Ade is determined to find his father's killer and make sure they pay for what they did. He thinks getting into politics is the best way to make it happen. When Ade became a member of the Like- Minded Political Party, he got connected with people who thought like him and had the same goals. Thanks to Dr. Sukhdev Singh for making him a part of the party, Ade now has a way to get into politics and use the party's help to fight for what he believes in.

Ade knows that politics can give him the power and influence he needs to confront the powerful people involved in his father's murder. Being part of the Like-Minded Political Party, Ade can use the party's channels and ways, to fight for justice and make sure the ones responsible for his father's death are caught...

Moreover, Ade's reason for joining the Like- Minded Political Party is based on his strong dedication to pursuing fairness, not just for his own family, but also for the wider community impacted by similar acts of violence and lawlessness. By using his influence within the party, Ade hopes to make the voices of those who are ignored, louder and fight for changes in the system that tackle the underlying reasons behind crime and corruption.

Ade, who is part of the Like- Minded Political Party, uses smart tactics to push the police to investigate his father's murder faster. With the help of his connections in the party, Ade gets important information and tools that help him dig deeper into what happened to his dad.

With the help of his friends from the political party, Ade discovers important information that links a well-known contract killer named Solomon Singh to his father's murder. By working hard to investigate and teaming up with the party members, Ade finds out that Mr. Ratan Singh, a famous teak wood businessman in Imphal, is believed to have hired Solomon Singh.

Mr. Ratan Singh does more than just sell teak wood - he's also involved in illegal stuff like selling drugs and smuggling gold. Even though lots of people know about his crimes, like politicians, big contractors, and even high-up police officers, nobody speaks up or does anything to stop him. This new information shows how everything is connected in the corrupt and criminal world of Imphal. Ratan Singh is right in the middle of it all. Ade understands that finding out the truth about his father's murder won't be easy. He'll have to face dangerous enemies and deal with people who have their own hidden agendas.

Even though there are many difficult obstacles in front of him, Ade is not discouraged and keeps fighting for justice. With new information and the support of his friends in the Like- Minded Political Party, he is getting ready to face corruption directly. He is determined to uncover the plot behind his father's murder and make sure the people responsible are held accountable.

Ade wanted to find justice for his dad's murder, so he went to Sukhdev Singh with a proof that Solomon Singh was involved. But Sukhdev Singh didn't care and wouldn't help. Ade was confused and upset, wondering why Sukhdev didn't want to help with something so important. As Ade digs further into Sukhdev Singh's past, he uncovers disturbing facts about his so-called friend. It turns out that Sukhdev Singh is not just involved in illegal activities, but is also participating in shady business transactions with the same people, who were involved in Ade's father's murder. This shocking discovery causes Ade to lose faith in Sukhdev and leaves him feeling betrayed and disappointed. Ade discovers that Sukhdev Singh is actually working with the evil guys he's trying to stop, making his quest for justice even harder. Despite Sukhdev's betrayal, Ade remains determined to uncover the truth and ensure that those responsible for his father's death are brought to justice.

One calm Sunday evening, Ade is relaxing at home with his family, enjoying the cozy feeling of being surrounded by familiar things. Suddenly, their peaceful time is interrupted by a group of police officers showing up at their door. The family is confused and worried as the officers come closer to Ade and tell him about a complaint that has been made against him.

Ade was really surprised when everything suddenly changed. So, Ade decided to ask the officers for more information about the complaint and where it came from. The police officers stayed calm and serious, and they told Ade to come with them to the police station for more questions and explanations. Even though Ade tried to argue and figure out what was going on, the officers didn't change their minds. Ade had no other option but to do what they said.

As Ade hesitantly goes with the police officers to the police station, a feeling of worry and uneasiness hangs in the air. His family, especially his mom, is overwhelmed with sadness and fear, their voices filled with pleas for assistance and desperation. The tears streaming down Ade's mom's face are a powerful reminder of how serious the situation is and the unknown future that awaits them. Feeling sad and confused, Ade goes to the police station with the officers, not knowing what will happen next. The road ahead looks tough, making Ade and his family worried about, what will happen when they get there.

In the police station, Ade is shocked to hear a surprising accusation. The officers explain the situation, and Ade is a bit confused and unsure about the seriousness of the accusations. They mention that someone was caught with illegal drugs and claimed Ade was involved as a messenger who was paid. Ade keeps saying he didn't do anything wrong and doesn't know anything about the person who got caught or the illegal stuff they're talking about. But even though he keeps saying he's innocent, the police still thought he's involved.

As tensions grow and feelings get intense, Ade is stuck in a whirlwind of not knowing what will happen next. The burden of the false accusation weighs heavily on him, making people doubt and suspect his character. Even though Ade tries his best to defend himself and prove the accusations wrong, nobody listens to him. The officers arrest him anyway, making him feel powerless and unfairly targeted by the very people, who are supposed to bring justice and keep innocent people safe. Ade's future is uncertain now, making him feel a combination of unfairness and betrayal. When he's being taken away with handcuffs, his pleas of innocence could be heard echoing in the station, revealing the flaws and unfairness of the justice system.

The next day, Ade's mom got a big surprise when a stranger she had never met before showed up at their door. She felt really nervous but still invited the stranger inside, even though she had no idea why he had come to visit.

When the stranger talks to Thoinu, his words are really scary and make her feel very uneasy. He gives her a scary choice, saying he'll drop the case if Ade stops trying to find justice for his dad's murderer. Thoinu gets worried and scared for her son after hearing that.

Ade mother, Thoinu is in a tough spot right now. She's feeling all mixed up because she wants to protect her family, but she also wants to make sure her husband's death is properly investigated. The things that the mysterious attacker said left her feeling extremely anxious and unsure about what steps to take next. It's like a big storm of confusion and uncertainty hovering over them, making everything even harder to figure out. Finally, she accepts the condition of the stanger. After the stranger went away, Ade's mother started wondering about what the frightening message meant. She had to make an extremely difficult decision which made her feel really torn. She wasn't sure if she should keep her family safe or uncover the truth about her husband's death. Thoinu, Ade's mother bravely decides to talk to Ade about something really scary. When she tells him what happened, Ade goes from being shocked, to not believing it and feeling really sad. As a result, Ade was set free from the jail.

Ade's mother believes that Imphal is not a safe place for her two sons to live. Moving back to their old Thangmeiband village is a major decision for their family. It involves changing their lives completely, by leaving their current home and returning to their previous residence. Ade, and Ryan felt a mix of emotions when they found out their mom's choice. The fact that they were sad and down in the dumps, really proves how much it impacted them. Ade and Ryan, as brothers shared a bond that makes this decision extra important to them. They have to handle their own emotions while also thinking about how it will impact each other and their whole family.

Ade and Ryan might be feeling really sad and down because they felt they're losing something and they don't know what's going to happen next. It's hard for them to accept the fact that they have to leave their home, their friends, neighbors, and everything they're used to. It's also kind of scary for them to think about going back to their old village. They might feel a mix of happy memories, excitement, and worry as they remember things from their past.

Ade was feeling sad and not happy as he sat in his room. All of a sudden, he remembered his old friend, the Teak tree. He made up his mind to ask the tree for some help. Ade was totally shocked when the furniture in his room actually answered his request for assistance. This proves that Ade never thought the objects in his room could come alive and talk to him, which made the whole thing feel weird and surprising. Ade's surprise shows just how amazing and unusual this situation is, setting the stage for a moment of realization and understanding.

Ade: "Who are you?"

Furniture: "I'm your old buddy. I'm here to lend a hand."

Ade: "So you're made from the Teak tTree, my old pal."

Furniture: "That's right, Ade."

Ade: "I'm really upset. My family is going through a tough time and no one is coming to help."

Furniture: "Can I be of any assistance?"

Ade tells the whole story to the furniture.

Furniture: "Don't worry, Ade. But I can't help because I'm just a tree. I suggest you listen to your mother's advice and return to your original Thangmeiband Village to protect the small tree growing in the Cheirou Ching Forest."

Ade: "But how will that help my family?"

Furniture: "Your mother knows best, Ade. By returning to your village and protecting the small tree, you are not only preserving your family's heritage but also ensuring a sustainable future for your community. The Cheirou Ching Forest holds the key to your family's prosperity and well-being."

Ade: "I never realized the importance of that small tree. I always thought it was just another part of the forest."

Furniture: "That small tree represents the resilience and strength of your family. It is a symbol of hope and growth. By protecting it, you are safeguarding your family's legacy and ensuring a brighter future for generations to come."

Ade: "You're right, my old buddy. I need to listen to my mother's advice and take action. I will return to Thangmeiband Village and do whatever it takes to protect that small tree."

Furniture: "That's the spirit, Ade! Always remember, you have companions with you on this venture. Your family, your community, and even I, your old buddy, will be there to support you at every step of the way."

Ade: "Thank you, my old pal. I have no idea how I would manage without your guidance and help. I will make sure to fulfill my duty and protect the small tree in the Cheirou Ching Forest."

After years of living in the bustling city, Ade finally made up his mind to return to his roots. He longed to reconnect with his village friends, who had remained in Thangmeiband Village. With a renewed sense of purpose, Ade shared his decision with his mother and brother Ryan, who were equally thrilled to embark on this journey. Ade's family got ready for the trip with excitement. They carefully packed their things, making sure they had all that they needed for their journey. They collected supplies like food, water, and camping equipment, understanding that the way to the village would be challenging. Each day, they became more and more excited, looking forward to the time they would arrive in Thangmeiband Village.

As the day of departure arrived, Ade's family set off on their journey. On the way, they encountered the wonders of nature that surrounded them. Majestic waterfalls cascaded down rocky cliffs, their soothing sounds providing a respite from the physical exertion. Vibrant flora and fauna adorned the landscape, painting a picturesque scene that seemed straight out of a fairytale. Ade's family marveled at the beauty that enveloped them, feeling a deep connection to the land they called home.

Finally, after days of perseverance, they reached the outskirts of Thangmeiband Village. The sight of familiar faces and the warm embrace of their loved ones filled their hearts with joy. The villagers welcomed them with open arms, eager to share their stories and the wisdom that had been passed down through generations.

Thangmeiband village is really important to Ade because it's like the center of the forest that took care of him and his family for a long time. Ade wants to go back to his family's old home to feel connected to the land and the customs that make him who he really is. He wants to keep the forest safe because he feels a strong urge to take care of nature, which he had learned while growing up and spending time with the Teak Tree.

Ade takes the initiative to establish a village protection force for safeguarding the Cheirou Ching Forest. Recognizing that protecting the forest requires collective effort and community engagement, Ade takes the lead in mobilizing the youth of the village and garnering their support for the cause. Ade makes sure that everyone in the village understands, how important it is to protect the forest by talking to all the young people. They have meetings and discussions, to get everyone involved and interested in the project. By working together and talking openly, they figure out what they need to do, to keep the forest safe. They all agree to work together towards this goal. Creating a special group to protect the forest shows how much the villagers care about saving Cheirou Ching's natural beauty. By working together in an organized way, they can act quickly to keep the forest safe from harm.

The village protection force keeps an eye on the forest every day to stop malpractices... They make sure only the right people can go in there, so no one can cut down trees or hurt animals. In general, Ade is really proactive and he made a group called the village protection force to take care of the Cheirou Ching Forest. This shows that he cares a lot about the community and wants to keep the forest safe for everyone, now and in the future. They all work together to make sure that the villagers and the environment can live together peacefully. They want to make sure that this special forest will be protected for a long time.

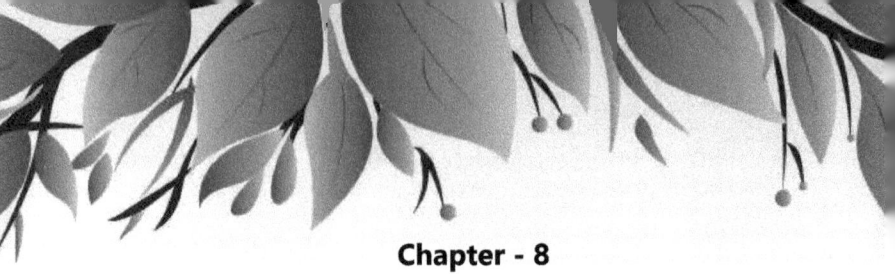

Chapter - 8

Confrontation with Illegal Loggers

When the sun goes down and the trees are covered in long shadows, there are some sneaky people hiding in the shadows too. They have bad intentions and are doing things secretly. At night, the bad loggers go into the Cheirou Ching forest quietly, their feet not making any noise on the ground covered with leaves. They wear masks to cover their faces and are determined to earn money by chopping down trees. They see the forest as a way to get rich, not as a home for the many different animals.

As they make their way through the thick bushes, the evil loggers pick out the big trees they want, looking for the ones with expensive wood. They start chopping away with their axes and chainsaws, the loud noise filling the air. Every time they swing their axe, it's like a sad sound spreading through the forest, showing how much damage they're causing. The noise of trees crashing down echoes all around the forest, breaking the peaceful quiet that used to fill the Cheirou Ching. Birds quickly fly away from their resting spots, their sweet melodies replaced by the loud chaos of destruction. Tiny creatures run in every direction; their cozy homes destroyed by the never-ending attack of the loggers.

The loggers don't care about the law and keep cutting down trees in the forest. They only care about making money and don't even feel sorry for what they're doing. They chop down trees without thinking, just wanting to get rich and not caring about nature. The Village Protection Force in Thangmeiband Village is always watching out for any trouble in the forest. They know how important it is to protect the Cheirou Ching, so they are prepared to fight off any danger that comes their way. With their strong determination and love for nature, they are ready to keep their home safe no matter what.

Suddenly, a sound in the bushes grabs the Protection Force's attention. They swiftly and silently navigate through the forest, moving closer to the source of the disturbance. The noise of axes and chainsaws grows louder as they get nearer, fueling their determination to halt the intruders and prevent further damage.

The Protection Force quickly surrounds the illegal loggers, surprising them and stopping their attack on the forest. Wearing masks, the loggers stand still, realizing they have been found out. The villagers demand answers from the intruders, speaking with confidence and determination. The illegal loggers got caught in the act, and now they're trying to explain why they did it. They say they didn't know about the laws that protect the forest, and thus they're asking for forgiveness. But the Protection Force won't give in to their lies. They're determined to protect the Cheirou Ching, no matter what.

As things get more intense, a fight starts between the loggers and the villagers, and you can hear the sounds of the struggle throughout the forest. Even though there are more loggers and villagers, the Protection Force doesn't back down. They are determined to keep the forest safe and thus won't give up.

Finally, the evil loggers are caught and stopped, and their tools of destruction are taken away as proof of their violations... Now that the danger is gone for now, the Protection Force focuses on fixing the forest and works really hard to undo the damage caused by the intruders.

In the middle of all the craziness, all the evil guys ran away, except for one guy named Phillip Singh. While the brave villagers were fighting against the mean illegal loggers, they managed to catch Phillip. It may seem like a small victory, but it's actually a huge deal.

Phillip Singh, is now in the custody of the vigilant villagers. The villagers see Phillip's capture as a real symbol of their strength and determination to protect their forest from people, who want to use it for their own benefit. Phillip starts to realize how serious the situation is, when he sees the results of what he did. He understands that he got caught in the act and can't deny that he took part in the illegal logging that harmed the forest. Despite feeling guilty, he still has a strong sense of rebellion inside him. When the villagers question Phillip, trying to get answers and make him take the responsibility, he finds it hard to stay calm. He talks quickly, telling a mix of lies and half-truths in a frantic attempt to avoid the consequences of what he did. But deep down, he realizes that it's too late - he knows that he will face the consequences for hurting others.

The news that Phillip Singh was actually sent by Sukhdev Singh, who lives in Imphal, shocked everyone in the village. Ade Singh and the other villagers didn't waste any time and quickly handed Phillip over to the nearby police station. This brave and determined action shows their dedication to seeking justice for their community and making sure that those who are responsible for the illegal activities in the forest are held accountable for what they've done. Sukhdev Singh found out about Phillip's arrest and wanted to help. He attempted to free Philip Singh by giving money to the police officer. The release of Phillip Singh from jail, facilitated by Sukhdev's illicit dealings with the police, serves as a stark reminder of the challenges they face in their quest for justice. Ade and the other villagers were really disappointed when Phillip was set free. It made them realize how hard it would be to fight against powerful people, who are only interested in their own benefits. However, this setback only made them more determined to keep fighting, no matter what challenges they face. They understood that the journey ahead won't be easy, but they are determined to protect their community and the way they live.

Sukhdev Singh, a businessman cum politician was well aware of the influential position held by Ade as the leader of the Village Protection Force. Recognizing the potential threat that Ade's leadership posed to his business, Sukhdev Singh devised a cunning plan to safeguard his own interests. Realizing that if Ade were to rally the villagers and lead them, their collective power could potentially disrupt the smooth functioning of his business operations. Sukhdev Singh understood that he needed to prevent Ade's idea from gaining traction within the community. With a keen eye for identifying dissenting voices, Sukhdev Singh embarked on a mission to find individuals in the village who were opposed to Ade's idea. He sought out those who had grievances or differing opinions, and skillfully approached them with an enticing offer - money.

Using his financial resources as leverage, Sukhdev Singh strategically paid these individuals to voice their opposition to Ade's leadership and his proposed plans for the Village Protection Force. By exploiting their discontent and providing them with monetary incentives, he successfully sowed seeds of doubt and dissent among the villagers. Through his calculated actions, Sukhdev Singh aimed to weaken Ade's influence and undermine his credibility within the community. By fueling division and discord, he hoped to prevent the villagers from uniting under Ade's leadership, thereby safeguarding his own business interests.

Sukhdev Singh was not only causing trouble among the villagers, but he was also coming up with a sneaky plan to help himself, while pretending to help the community. He knew that some villagers were not happy with Ade's leadership and wanted to see the village improve. Sukhdev took advantage of their desire for progress to get what he really wanted.

Sukhdev had a great idea to make the Cheirou Ching forest better. He wanted to cut down the old teak trees so that they could have space and build important things for the community, like a school, hospital, and market. Sukhdev knew that the villagers wanted modern things and a better life, so he talked about how this plan would make the village better and help it grow. He was really smart and had a big vision for the future! Sukhdev cleverly made himself look like a hero for progress, suggesting a really good idea to help the village. People who believed in a better tomorrow, liked his plan and were ready to help with projects that claimed to help everyone in the village. Sukhdev actually wanted to chop down the ancient teak trees in the woods to make money from selling the wood, caring more about his own wallet than the people in the village. He tried to trick everyone by pretending that his plan was for the village's benefit, but in reality, he just wanted to take advantage of their resources. Even though Sukhdev tried to convince some villagers with his fancy words and promises of progress, Ade stayed alert and saw through Sukhdev's sneaky plan. He knew that Sukhdev's idea would harm the forest and make it hard for the village to keep its resources.

Ade and his friends from the village were on a mission to uncover Sukhdev Singh's evil actions... They knew it was a serious job. They were determined and never gave up. They carefully followed Sukhdev Singh's actions and collected proof to show that their suspicions were true. They wanted to reveal the truth that was hidden behind Sukhdev Singh's fake image of being respectable.

They meticulously observed every move of Sukhdev Singh, carefully, documented his actions and collected evidence to support their claims. They knew that in order to reveal the truth, they needed concrete proof that would shatter Sukhdev Singh's fake respectable image. One fateful day, as they were discreetly following Sukhdev Singh, Ade and his friends stumbled upon a shocking scene. They saw Sukhdev Singh meeting Pritam Singh, a notorious drug user, at a nearby hotel. Their hearts raced as they witnessed Sukhdev handing over a wad of cash to Pritam, who swiftly left the premises. It was clear that something sinister was going on, and Ade Singh and his friends were determined to uncover the truth.

Later that night, as Sukhdev Singh made his way towards Imphal City, tragedy struck the village. A massive fire broke out in the Cheirou Ching forest where teak tree grew, threatening to engulf everything in its path. The villagers rallied together, desperately trying to extinguish the flames and save their homes and livelihoods. Amidst the chaos, Ade noticed that Pritam Singh was nowhere to be found.

The next day, the devastating news reached the village. Pritam Singh had tragically died from a drug overdose near their community. Ade's suspicions were further fueled, as he couldn't shake the feeling that this was all a part of Sukhdev Singh's plan. It seemed too coincidental that Pritam would meet his demise, just after their encounter with Sukhdev. Determined to uncover the truth, Ade and his friends delved deeper into their investigation. They discovered a web of deceit and corruption that Sukhdev Singh had carefully woven around himself. It became evident that he was using Pritam as a pawn in his illegal activities, manipulating him for his own gain. Armed with their evidence, Ade and his friends decided it was time to confront Sukhdev Singh and expose his true nature to the rest of the village. They organized a community meeting, where they presented their findings and revealed the extent of Sukhdev's deceit. The villagers were shocked and outraged, realizing that they had been misled.

After one month, Ade and the Villager were shocked to hear that Sukhdev Singh had been killed. Ade pondered who might have done it. He understood that there were people behind this crime, but he also knew they were not just regular folks. He figured it would be hard to capture them.

Sukhdev Singh's death wasn't just an ordinary happening; it was a huge shock that shook the whole village. Everyone, including Ade, was completely stunned and confused as they tried to understand what Sukhdev's death meant. But even in the midst of all the confusion, Ade couldn't help but feel that there was something fishy about Sukhdev's murder. Ade had a feeling that Sukhdev's death wasn't just some random thing or a fight between friends. He understood that it was actually a big plan made by powerful people. This made him think there was something even more sneaky going on, with secret reasons and hidden plans. Ade was facing some really scary thoughts, but he understood that finding out what really happened to Sukhdev, wouldn't be a walk in the park. It would take bravery, a strong will, and the guts to face the criminals hiding in their village... But Ade wasn't going to back down; he was determined to figure out the truth about Sukhdev's death, no matter what.

Ade was really adamant to figure out what really happened to Sukhdev Singh. He was motivated by personal reasons and also wanted to help his community. Ade wasn't just looking for justice for Sukhdev; he also wanted to find out who killed his dad and make sure the Cheirou Ching forest stayed safe.

The Sukhdev's murder and his father's death were something Ade couldn't ignore. Both incidents were surrounded by mystery and done by people who wanted to benefit from the teak tree forest. Ade knew there was a dark link between the two events, and he was determined to find out the truth, no matter what it took. After understanding how important it was, Ade gathered all the villagers for a meeting to talk about what they should do next. They talked about how they could keep their community safe and stop more violence from happening. Finally, they all agreed that they had to make security stronger and build up their defenses.

During the meeting, they made an important choice. They decided to have strict rules for checking people, who wanted to enter the Cheirou Ching forest through their village. They knew that the forest was very important and some people might want to do crimes there. By making everyone go through a verification process before going into the forest, they wanted to find and stop anyone who seemed suspicious. They also wanted to make sure that nobody did anything in the forest without permission. Also, Ade Singh and the villagers knew it was important to have someone in charge nearby, to keep things in order. They thought it would be a good idea to ask the Forest Office to set up a small base close to their village. This way, it would help stop, the wicked people from causing trouble and make it easier to respond quickly if there were any safety concerns. Having a Forest Office base nearby would not only provide a sense of security for the villagers, but it would also serve as a deterrent for any potential troublemakers. Ade and the villagers understood the importance of having a presence of authority in their community to maintain peace and order.

By having a base close to their village, the Forest Office would be able to respond promptly to any safety concerns or emergencies that may arise. This would ensure that the villagers have access to the necessary support and resources in times of need. Furthermore, having a base nearby would also allow better communication and coordination between the villagers and the Forest Office. This partnership would strengthen the relationship between the two parties and create a sense of unity in working towards the common goal of protecting the village and its inhabitants. Overall, establishing a small base for the Forest Office near the village would not only enhance the safety and security of the community, but it would also foster a sense of collaboration and cooperation among all parties involved. It was a proactive step taken by Ade and the villagers to ensure the well-being of their community.

Ade is causing a lot of trouble for the teak business people in Imphal. They are really worried because Ade wants to reveal all the malpractices they have been indulged into... To protect themselves, the teak business people are planning to do something really drastic. They are so desperate that they are even considering teaming up with a stranger, maybe even a professional assassin, to get rid of Ade. During their private meeting, the rich teak businessman hands over a large sum of money to the person they hired to carry out a terrible task. They gave Rs 5 lakh upfront and assure to provide additional funds once the job is completed. This payment serves as a major incentive for the hired individual, to carry out the nefarious deed.

According to their strategy, the teak business leaders design a clever scheme to fool Ade into believing that they are innocent. They decide to hold a special event to honor those who work hard to save the environment. Knowing Ade's love for the forest, they nominate him for an award and share the news in the local newspapers. When Ade learns about the nomination, he is thrilled and can't wait to attend the ceremony. The teak business leaders, driven by their desperation to maintain their innocence, meticulously planned every detail of their scheme to deceive Ade. They knew that Ade's love for the forest made him vulnerable to their manipulations, and thus, they decided to exploit his passion for their own advantage. With their cunning minds at work, the teak business leaders devised a plan to organize a grand event that would honor individuals dedicated to environmental protection. They carefully selected a venue that exuded elegance and charm, ensuring that it would captivate Ade's attention. The news of this prestigious event was strategically leaked to the local newspapers, creating a buzz within the community.

As the news of the event spread like wildfire, Ade's name emerged as a prominent nominee for the coveted award.

The teak business leaders, aware of Ade's genuine commitment to preserving the environment, believed that this nomination would not only deceive him but also serve as a distraction from their true intentions. They skillfully manipulated the situation, making Ade believe that he was being recognized for his unwavering efforts.

Ade, upon discovering his nomination, was overwhelmed with excitement and anticipation. The prospect of attending the ceremony and being acknowledged for his dedication filled him with joy. Unbeknownst to him, the teak business leaders had already set their plan in motion, ensuring that Ade's journey to Thailand would be an integral part of their scheme.

The organizers of the award function, acting as the teak business leaders' pawns, presented Ade with a beautifully crafted certificate, symbolizing his supposed achievement. To further deceive him, they included a complimentary trip to Thailand, a country renowned for its lush forests and breathtaking landscapes. Ade's heart swelled with gratitude as he received the unexpected gift, unaware of the sinister plot unfolding around him.

The teak business leaders, with their intricate web of deceit, had already orchestrated the assassin's arrival in Thailand. The assassin, equipped with the knowledge of Ade's hotel and room number, had meticulously planned every step to ensure the success of their malevolent mission. Unbeknownst to Ade, his fate had already been sealed.

Upon his arrival in Thailand, Ade settled into his hotel room, blissfully unaware of the impending tragedy. The teak business leaders had ensured that his room was meticulously prepared, creating an illusion of safety and comfort. Ade, oblivious to the danger lurking nearby, immersed himself in the beauty of his surroundings, unaware of the darkness that awaited him.

As Ade, unsuspecting and filled with excitement, arrived in Thailand, was completely unaware of the lurking danger that awaited him. Little did he know that his every move was being meticulously observed by the killer, who had already settled into his room, shrouded in darkness and secrecy. The sun dipped below the horizon, casting an eerie glow over the city as nightfall descended upon the hotel. Ade, tired from the day's adventures, retired to his room, oblivious to the malevolent presence lurking just a wall away. The air was thick with an unsettling tension, as the killer prepared to execute the meticulously planned act of violence.

In the dark of night, when the world was silent, the killer crept inside Ade's bed. His heart pounded with a mix of anticipation and malice, his hands trembling with the weight of the sinister intentions. The room, once a sanctuary of comfort and tranquility, now became a chilling crime scene, destined to forever hold the secrets of Ade's untimely demise.

The killer quickly and carefully stopped Ade from making any noise, taking away their lively energy in a flash. The room, once filled with life, now became a haunting testament to the darkness that resided within the killer's soul. The echoes of Ade's final moments reverberated through the walls, forever etching a sense of dread into the very fabric of the hotel. As the sun rose over the horizon, casting its warm rays upon the city, the hotel staff discovered the lifeless body of Ade, a tragic victim of a meticulously planned murder. Panic and disbelief spread like wildfire, as the realization of a killer lurking among them took hold. The once idyllic hotel now became a crime scene, teeming with investigators, searching for any shred of evidence that could lead them to the elusive killer.

Ade's tragic death sends shockwaves through the community, leaving his mother and loved ones devastated. His untimely demise serves as a grim reminder of the lengths to which those in power will go to silence dissent and protect their vested interests. Despite Ade's noble intentions and tireless efforts to expose corruption and protect the environment, his life is cut short by the greed and ruthlessness of those he sought to oppose.

His mother's lamentation reflects the bitter reality that in a world driven by greed and corruption, good deeds often go unrewarded, and justice remains elusive.

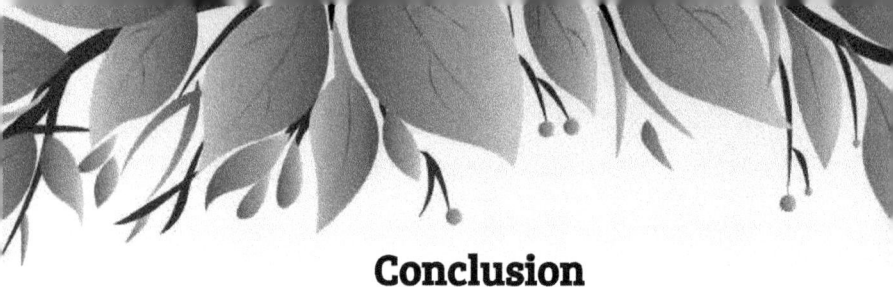

Conclusion

In the shadowy world of greed and corruption, Ade's story serves as a poignant reminder of the enduring struggle between good and evil. His unwavering commitment to justice and environmental preservation stood as a beacon of hope amidst the darkness of illicit dealings and criminal enterprises. Throughout his journey, Ade encountered numerous challenges and faced formidable adversaries, yet he never wavered in his pursuit of truth and righteousness. His relentless efforts to uncover the truth behind his father's murder and protect the Cheirou Ching forest epitomized the resilience of the human spirit in the face of adversity.

However, Ade's noble quest ultimately ended in tragedy, as he fell victim to the ruthless machinations of those who sought to silence him. His untimely demise served as a stark reminder of the dangers inherent in challenging powerful interests and exposing corruption. Yet, even in death, Ade's legacy endured. His unwavering courage and determination inspired others to carry on his fight for justice and environmental stewardship. The villagers of Thangmeiband Village, galvanized by Ade's sacrifice, continued to protect their forest home and uphold his ideals. In the end, Ade Singh's story serves as a testament to the power of one individual to ignite change and inspire others to stand up against injustice. Though his journey was cut short, his legacy lives on, a testament to the enduring impact of courage, integrity, and the unwavering pursuit of justice.

www.ingramcontent.com/pod-product-compliance
Lightning Source LLC
LaVergne TN
LVHW061344080526
838199LV00094B/7346